BE STILL
AND KNOW
THAT I AM GOD

A NOVEL

PAMELA YOUNG

Be Still And Know That I am God
Pamela Young

3rd Edition

Copyright© 2025 CAVU Publishing

ISBN 978-0-9897360-4-6

Cover Image by Igoe Zh/Shutterstock

For George…
The wind beneath my wings

REVIEWS OF BE STILL

Thank you....absolutely beautiful..we are in very troubled times.."GO OUT AND TELL THE THE WORLD" No matter what be people of faith.....Be still and know that I AM God....I will be with you until the end of time... .

— LAURIE LACINA

What a timely book. I absolutely love how the author brought out the reality of who's in charge here.) We think we are, never realizing what we do or who we hurt to gain importance, wealth and notoriety. When the dust finally clears, we will discover how puny and insignificant we really are. The book flows so smoothly and it kept me in constant curiosity as to what would happen next. The research that went into the writing of this, is phenomenal. What with our disastrous economy and problems around the world today, the author is right on target.

— SHARON ROSS

Great story. Very uplifting. Don't want to spoil the ending, but it was fantastic. Very well written. Look forward to reading more from this author.

— LINDA

Very good book. I think it is a very plausible scenario for our world. It kept me interested to the end.

— JAN DENBY

I have just finished drying my tears after reading Be Still. What a timely, beautifully written, and thought provoking novel! Everyone should order a copy from Amazon immediately! All of us can relate to either Amanda, whose anger at God meant alienation from her family, or to her father, whose unwavering faith was a constant, or to other characters from varying backgrounds and faiths. Regardless of your religion, or lack thereof, you will be inspired by Be Still. What an awesome read! This book is a winner! KUDOS to Pamela Young!

— MARY FREEMAN

What I look for and enjoy most in a book are well developed characters, scenery, action, and anticipation of what will happen next. This book has it all and I enjoyed it so much. It brings us back to what's really important---and we ALL need to be there!! Especially in these difficult times. When I put the book down, and until the next opportunity for reading came along, I found myself thinking about what I had read. When I finished the book, that process continued, and I'm sure it will for a very long time. This is a wonderful, timely, and thought-provoking book. Meaningful on so many levels.

— C. SANDOZ

In reading this book I am struck by how real life it is. This could happen. The author, Pamela Young has woven such a rich story about greed, selfishness and the lack of God in our lives. Of course, in our current world conditions the message in this book is dead on. It gave me hope and really helped me revisit my faith. This book is fabulous, and I can't wait for more work from this author.

— A. GUSTAFSON

What a great read I loved this book! I am a fan from now on of Pamela Young! This book was so easy to read YEA!

— K. ELLIOTT

Be Still was such an engaging book. I didn't want to put the book down. I thoroughly enjoyed it. The storyline was very believable, current, and inspiring.

— PAIGE SCHAFER

"O come behold what wondrous works
Jehovah's hand has wrought,
Come, see what desolation great
He on the earth has brought.
To utmost ends of all the earth
He causes war to cease,
The weapons of the strong destroyed
He makes abiding peace.
Be still and know that I am God
O'er all exalted high,
The subject nations of the earth
My name shall magnify.
Our Lord of Hosts is on our side
Our safety is secure,
The God of Jacob is for us
A refuge strong and sure."

— PSALMS 46 ORIGINAL TRINITY HYMNAL NO. 37

PROLOGUE

It was just after 9:00 a.m. when the St. Charles Streetcar stopped near Lafayette Cemetery. The doors opened and an old woman carefully walked down the steps, carrying her basket filled with carnations and a plate of coconut macaroons.

"Are you making it okay, Miss Ellie?" the driver asked.

"Doing fine, Calvin, thank you," she replied.

"Well then, you have a real nice day today and I'll see you next week."

She smiled, "See you next week, Calvin."

It was the same conversation that they had every week. Calvin was a relatively new driver. He had only been on this route for the last five years. There had been four other drivers over the past twenty-five years and each one of them had held a special place in their hearts for Ellie LeBeaux. At eighty-nine she was almost as spry as she had been at sixty, and always had a kind word and a genuine interest in everyone she met.

There were dark clouds overhead as she walked down the tree-lined streets toward the cemetery. The earthy aroma of last night's rain permeated the air. She was going to visit her husband, Reginald, and her two babies as she did every Monday. Normally she would pass people in the neighborhoods or tourists visiting the Garden District, but today was unusually quiet and she could actually hear the leaves rustling in the trees.

As she entered the cemetery with its raised tombs, she stopped in front of the one marked *LeBeaux*. Her husband's name was listed on the top with his birth and death dates. Underneath was the name of her son, Reginald Jr., and finally the name of her daughter Missy, who had died when she was eighteen months old of scarlet fever. "I'm back, my precious ones," she said as she removed last week's withered carnations and the empty plate.

Opening her basket, she added the new spice scented white flowers to the vase and then set out the plate of freshly baked macaroons. "I know how much you love these," she said, rearranging the cookies on the plate. "They're especially good today. I think that extra little bit of vanilla made all the difference. Sally stopped by yesterday. She's doing fine and she said Robert was just accepted to Tulane. She said he wants to be a doctor. I told her it's a good thing to have a doctor in this family, especially with the cost of medical care these days."

She smiled and continued, "He is a good boy, Reginald. I know you would have really loved him. He looks like you—so handsome—and he has the same sense of humor that Reginald Jr. had. I'll bet Reggie is still telling you all his stories. Remember how he used to bring us to tears? We laughed so hard." She was quiet then, thinking about the fun they all used to have. She reached up and put her hand against the gravestone. "I miss you all so much, but I know God is taking good care of you." She bowed her head and said a quiet prayer for each one of her loved ones. "Amen," she said quietly and then looked up at their names. "I'll see you next week. I love you." She lightly kissed her fingers and touched the gravestone.

As she turned to leave, a breeze swept through the cemetery and swirled leaves over the tops of the tombstones and along the path. She gathered her basket and slowly began her short journey back to St. Charles Avenue.

"Ellie."

She looked around. No one was in the cemetery. She knew she must be hearing things, so she continued her walk.

"Ellie." She stopped. This time she knew she heard something. She searched the cemetery until finally she saw someone up ahead. Ellie walked closer, thinking it might be someone who worked there, but as she neared the man, she realized it was someone she had never seen before. He was sitting on one of the tombs. As she approached, she saw that he had wings. Her heart began to race. She looked at him, more in wonder than in fear. "Who are you?"

"Ellie, do not be afraid. God loves you and has chosen you to deliver a message. He wants you to tell them that the Lord, your God, has loved His people but they have not loved Him. He wants you to tell His people to prepare themselves for their time is at hand."

Ellie was speechless as the angel came over to her. He stroked her cheek with the back of his finger and smiled at her. "He loves you, Ellie," he repeated. Then he slowly disappeared before her eyes.

CHAPTER ONE

A soft rain fell on St. Peter's Square as the faithful huddled under black umbrellas, awaiting word on the selection of the new Roman Catholic Church leader. The past two weeks had been an emotional roller coaster. First, the joyous celebration of Easter with the beloved pope, then the sheer horror as people heard shots during Mass and watched the pontiff fall back into the arms of his Cardinals.

Miraculously, he had survived the shooting. The doctors even had hope that he would recover, but two nights later, he became gravely ill and there was nothing the doctors could do to save him. The world heard sobs that continued through his funeral.

Amanda Fox adjusted her earpiece as she awaited the signal for her live feed. "As we go on the air tonight, the world awaits, with Rome and Roman Catholics everywhere watching the building behind me for the white smoke signaling the election of a new pope. The conclave has had five votes so far without success. I was told that the newly elected pope must have at least a sixty-six percent majority vote, but if that doesn't happen, a recent decree by the late pope established that a simple majority can elect the new pontiff. People have continued to pour into St. Peter's Square. In fact, Karl, it is unbelievable how many are here. Officials estimate the crowd at over five hundred thousand, and many have been here for several days."

Amanda heard a loud roar behind her. She looked back toward the Sistine Chapel, where white smoke was finally rising from the chimney. As thunderous applause came from the square, she turned back toward the camera. "It looks as if we have a new pope," she said as she held her earpiece in tighter in deference to the noise. The Sistine bells rang, their echoing peals almost deafening. "Let me step out of the way for a moment so you can sense the excitement of this crowd."

Pete Vargas, her cameraman, panned from the smoking chimney to the swinging bells over the rooftops to the cheering crowd. He saw movement on the pope's balcony and quickly zoomed in on the red-robed figure approaching the microphones.

"Habemus Papum," the Cardinal announced loudly. "We have a pope." A thunderous applause reverberated throughout the square as cheers went out from the crowd. He raised his hands to silence them. "The conclave has chosen as our new Holy Father Cardinal Josef Martinelli." Another thunderous applause rose from the crowd. The Cardinal once again waited for the crowd to be still. "He has chosen the name of James."

Through the roar of the crowd, Amanda shouted, "And so Pope James takes his place in history. The scene here is incredible. People are shouting and hugging each other and, I don't know if you can hear them, but they're chanting, 'Pope James, Pope James.' There's even a band beginning to play."

Amanda pressed her earpiece in even tighter to hear the question from Karl Morgan, the WNN news anchor. She looked at the camera with her clear blue eyes as she listened.

"That's right, Karl. Cardinal Martinelli was not the odds-on favorite because he is highly conservative. Many people I've spoken to this week have told me that the Catholic Church really needs more liberal leadership at this time to bring the church more into the twenty-first century. I recently spoke with Cardinal Martinelli, now the new pope, who discussed some of these issues with me."

As she was talking, both Amanda and Karl heard the director in their earpieces telling them to stretch the intro as a teaser of the cardinal's interview was being prepared for broadcast.

"Are you talking about abortion?" Karl asked her.

"Yes, abortion was one of the major issues we discussed, as well as his views on the ordination of women as priests, and also why the church has not had more tolerance for gay rights. I have to tell you, Karl, I found the cardinal to be a remarkable man. He has incredible inner strength and an unwavering faith, and yet his sensitivity to the needs of the people was amazing."

"I understand we've got a segment of that interview ready to roll," Karl said. Amanda watched the clip on her network monitor, followed by a close-up of the chapel balcony where several cardinals were forming a line.

The rain had stopped and afternoon sunlight glinted on Amanda's auburn hair as she turned to watch the newly elected pope come out on the balcony. Gone were the red robes of Cardinal Martinelli. Now, resplendent in white, stood Pope James. Another roar came from the crowd.

The newly elected Pope held his hands up to quiet the crowd and then clasped his hands. "Good people, I am your humble servant. By God's grace, I will serve you well." He then gave his first papal blessing to the people in the square and to the world. The crowd chanted, "Viva, James! Viva, James!"

"We will show the entire interview with the newly elected pope tonight at seven p.m. central time," Karl said. He added, "Amanda, I understand this was an exclusive interview?"

"That's right, Karl. Cardinal Mar...I should say Pope James is not a man who seeks publicity. He's a very modest man and I really feel that his election to the papacy was a complete surprise to him. In fact, he had high praises for several of the Cardinals who he felt would be excellent as the new leader of the Catholic Church."

"Well, that's an interview I'm sure none of us want to miss. Nice work, Amanda."

"Thanks, Karl. This is Amanda Fox live in Rome."

Pete switched off the camera and hefted it off his shoulder. "Timing is everything," she shouted to Pete. "Amazing that the vote came in live while we were rolling."

Pete rubbed his forehead with his sleeve, mopping the sweat. The lingering humidity was oppressive. "And even more amazing that the pope is none other than Cardinal Martinelli," he shouted over the din of the crowd.

"I know," Amanda said gleefully. "And we've got the interview with him. Exclusive interview." Amanda smiled. "How about dinner in an hour and we'll celebrate?"

"Got it," Pete said. "I'm looking forward to a shower. I'll meet you in the lobby."

The Hotel dei Consoli was at least a bit of calm amid the outside chaos. Amanda took off her jacket, tossed it on the bed, and sat in a very uncomfortable chair. She dialed WNN headquarters in Washington, D.C. "Hi, April. It's Amanda. Is Mark in?"

A moment later, Mark Laux, the executive producer of Amanda's news show, The Week-End Report with Amanda Fox, came on the line. "What can I say? The golden girl hits another one out of the park."

"Isn't that incredible, Mark? I mean, catching everything live would almost be enough, but Cardinal Martinelli becoming the new pope? Unbelievable, and what luck to have that interview all ready to go."

"Luck had nothing to do with it."

"Actually, it did. You know how everyone thought either Cardinal Fulton or Cardinal Martinez would be the next pope?

"Well, it was impossible to even get close to them since the press followed them everywhere," she said as she kicked off her shoes. "I knew I needed another angle, but I didn't know what it was. So, I thought I'd think about it over lunch and found this great little deli just off Vatican Square."

"Pizza, right?'

"No, but they have a great Tuscan Panzanella. Anyway, as I was waiting for lunch, Cardinal Martinelli wandered in. As he sat sipping his water, he turned and nodded to me. I smiled, went over to his table, and introduced myself. He knew who I was and invited me to join him.

"We had an incredible conversation about the church and its direction and so many other things. As we finished our lunches, I asked him if he might consent to a taped interview. He hesitated at first, but then agreed if I would report honestly, with absolutely no editing, his hope for the future of the church. And so," Amanda said at last, "you'll see the interview."

"I already have, and it's another Emmy winner. What will that make now? Five?"

Amanda was quiet. "It was just so terrific to talk to him, Mark. He really was genuine. It just seems that there is such sadness these days and, you know, he just seemed like hope personified."

"Yeah, I know what you mean. There was a shooting this morning in D.C. A postman, with a wife and four kids, was gunned down as he was leaving his home. The shooter was his fourteen-year-old pregnant girlfriend."

"Good grief, she's just a child."

"Yeah," Mark said. "One of his daughters was older than the girl."

"That's terrible."

"Yeah, someone should shoot him. Oh, wait," Mark said with a note of sarcasm. "She did."

"You're turning into a cynic."

"I know. It comes with the territory."

"Yep," Amanda said softly. "Well, try to have a better rest of the day. I'm meeting Pete for dinner to celebrate. I'll check back with you later."

"Good," Mark said. "Congratulations on a terrific day. Stay safe."

Amanda smiled as she closed her cell phone and thought about Mark. There was definitely a spark between them. Their relationship, though, was strictly business. She wouldn't allow anything else. She had made that mistake before. Mark, though, had become a friend almost since the moment he arrived at WNN over a year ago.

As an investigative reporter for KOMO News in Seattle, he had won three Emmys; however, a car accident that killed his wife and child turned his world upside down. Seattle held too many memories and he needed a change. When a senior news editor at WNN, who had known Mark for years, suggested that he come to Washington, D.C. and produce Amanda's news program, he accepted, thinking that a desk job was exactly what he needed.

Amanda glanced at her watch. She now had thirty minutes to shower, change into a fresh dress, and be down in the lobby to meet Pete.

Right at the appointed time, Amanda emerged from the elevator and saw that she was the first to arrive. She found a chair in the lobby and waited. As she glanced at the surrounding people, she noticed a woman dressed in a simple white blouse and a long, dark skirt. The woman kept staring at Amanda and finally started walking slowly toward her, stopping three feet in front of her. Amanda looked up in question. "Ciao."

The olive-skinned woman replied in halting English. "Are you Amanda Fox?"

Amanda smiled, realizing the woman had probably seen her on TV. "Yes, I am."

"I need you to help me," the woman said. "My brother has seen an angel, and no one believes him. You must talk to him," the woman continued urgently, "and you will see."

Through the course of her career, Amanda had encountered more than her share of unstable people and she could usually handle them without a problem. Religious fervor, though, was at its height in Rome at the moment, and the intense look in this woman's eyes made Amanda nervous. "Is your brother here in Rome?" she asked.

"No, no," the woman said. "No, he's home in Greece, in Kalymnos. You must come. I can take you there."

"I'm sorry, but who are you?" Amanda asked.

"Anna. Anna Kraikos. My brother is Niko Gravari. I have seen you on the television and I know you can help him. The town thinks he's crazy, but he's not. He won't leave his home or talk to anyone anymore, but I know he will talk to you. Something happened to him and he's scared. You can help him.

"Anna," Amanda said calmly, "I can't leave Rome. My job is here right now." She pulled a business card out of her jacket pocket and handed it to Anna. Write down your phone number and I'll see what I can do."

"Then you will come?" Anna asked pleadingly as she hurriedly wrote out her number and handed it back to Amanda.

"I'll see what I can do," Amanda repeated as she noticed Pete coming toward her.

"Thank you," Anna said as she grabbed Amanda's hand and squeezed hard. "Thank you." As Pete joined them, she glanced quickly at him, then turned and walked away.

"What was that all about?" Pete asked.

Amanda shook her head. "It's Rome. Religious zealots are every-where. A man came up to me yesterday to tell me he saw Jesus standing on the pope's balcony. Of course, no one else saw anything, but he was so convinced that he insisted I put him on camera. Didn't, of course, and he almost became violent."

She let out an exasperated breath as she shoved the business card back into her pocket. "This one saw an angel—Or at least she said her brother did. She wanted me to go with her to Greece." She smiled at Pete. "Glad you showed up when you did."

CHAPTER TWO

With his eyes closed, Reverend John Winters sat patiently in a large swivel chair as Doug, his makeup artist, worked his magic to ease the telltale signs of years of heavy drinking and smoking. In his mind, John was going over the sermon he was about to give not only his huge congregation, but to the millions of viewers who tuned in each Sunday morning. As he mentally rehearsed, he gave special emphasis to the words "and" and "but." He especially liked the way he said "glory," giving it three syllables. "Glory" was pedestrian, but "*gul-lor-ry*" was the mark of a master orator.

After thirty-three years in the pulpit, he knew all the tricks of the trade. It had taken him over thirty of those years to raise his Baton Rouge, Louisiana-based Spirit of Truth Church to the number one religious program on television. Because it was non-denominational, his church wasn't bound by the doctrines of any single religion. And the best thing about the Spirit of Truth Church was that he had total control.

"All set, sir," Doug said, turning the chair toward the mirror. Reverend John opened his hazel eyes and took a long look at himself, turning first to the left, then to the right. The years had not been good to him, but makeup was a wonderful thing. "Looks good," he said as he pulled off his bib and reached over for his hand-blown crystal bottle of Henry Jacque richly floral spicy parfum and dabbed a touch behind each ear. He loved the stuff. It just smelled rich and in fact it was, at $1000 a bottle. Feeling ready to perform, he eased his massive bulk from the chair. With Doug's help, he wriggled into his jacket and, taking one more look in the mirror, he leaned forward and adjusted his tie.

Although overweight, he found the custom-made Armani suit hid many flaws, and he was pleased with his appearance. Shoulders back, he carried himself with a commanding air of self-confidence as he waited for the cue to walk on stage.

Feeling the heat of the lights, he raised his hand and turned toward the camera and said, "Blessed be the Lord and blessed be all people who come to worship Him. Let us pray." All heads bowed as he continued. "We thank You, dear Lord, for this wonderful day. We thank You for Your generosity and for giving us all so much that we, in turn, can help others. Thank You, Father, for seeking those who will share their bounty with others in need around the world. Bless them and their gifts, returning tenfold what they give. We thank You in all of Your gul-lor-ry. Amen, amen."

CHAPTER THREE

The World News Network newsroom was in high gear the morning Amanda returned from Rome. During the evening, there had been a bombing, a thwarted terrorism attempt, and a murder. At 4:30 a.m. the bombing took place at an all-night abortion clinic just outside of New Orleans. The details were still sketchy, but at last count, sixteen were dead and three were missing. The terrorism attempt happened at 7:00 a.m. at the Lincoln Memorial, not five miles from the WNN headquarters. Police arrested four men, two with grenades in their pockets.

The murder involved a sixty-three-year-old police officer, only two years from retirement. Gunmen shot him down in front of the District police headquarters. There were no suspects at the moment and, surprisingly, given the location of the murder, no one had seen anything.

Amanda Fox stretched at her desk as she caught up on memos and the more trivial news of the morning. She had been back from Rome now for two days, but for some reason, she was still exhausted.

"Are we keeping you up?" She looked up to see Mark standing in her doorway, smiling.

"Okay, you caught me," she said with a laugh. "I don't know what it is. Either those flights are getting longer or I'm getting old, but flying isn't as much fun as it used to be."

Mark walked in and sat across from her. He was a rugged, yet youthful forty-five with a deep tan that contrasted with his blonde hair. Standing just over six feet, he was a good six inches taller than Amanda. "Well, if thirty-seven is old, then I must be ancient."

"How did you know I'm thirty-seven?"

Mark grinned. "I looked it up. One perk of being a boss." He sat back and laced his fingers over his chest. "So, the new pope is on the throne. Good reports, by the way. I remember Rome from my reporting days. It's always been a favorite city."

"Um," she agreed. "It is beautiful there, but it really was insane this time. Crowds were everywhere, and the range of emotions was phenomenal—the lowest of the lows and the highest of the highs. I think that's what was so hard this week, plus all the crazies that were there."

"What kind of crazies?"

"Well, one woman said a cross in her home bled when the pope died. She wanted me to interview her. So did the man who saw Jesus on the pope's balcony as the pope was dying. Millions of people were looking at that balcony, and that man was the only one who claimed to have seen Jesus. But my favorite was the woman who said her brother had not only seen, but had a conversation with, an angel."

"What?" Mark teased. "You don't believe in these things?"

She laughed. "Well, the Catholic in me certainly believes, but the reporter doesn't. We've both seen enough of the seedy side of the world to hold any huge illusions."

Mark's surprise was evident. "You're Catholic? Didn't know that. This week must have been very special to you."

"More unsettling, I think. Being Catholic was forced on me growing up. This may come as a real shock to you," she continued, smiling, "but I rebelled. I've been away from the church for years. My brother, though, became a priest. My mother would have loved to see his ordination. The church was so important to her, but she died when David and I were barely in our teens."

Amanda looked away for a moment and then back to Mark. "Anyway," she said, a little more forcefully than she intended, "it was an interesting week." She let out a breath. "Have to say, though, I didn't know what to make of that Greek lady. She was so insistent that her brother was telling the truth and wanted me to talk to him. I told her to write down the phone number and I would try to get hold of him. I've tried several times, but no one seems to answer."

"So, the story ends before it begins."

"You would think," replied Amanda, "until this came across my desk this morning." She handed Mark a wire about an angel sighting in New Orleans.

"Hum," he grunted as read it. "Coincidence?"

"I don't know," Amanda said. "Who's covering the abortion clinic bombing in New Orleans?"

"I was planning on sending Angela down."

"Why don't you send me instead, and while I'm there, I'll check out this angel lady," Amanda said as she stifled a yawn.

Mark smiled. "I think you're more tired than you know. Now you're chasing angels. Go home, you need sleep."

"Ah, sleeping's for amateurs. Got lots of stuff to do here before I head to New Orleans."

CHAPTER FOUR

Amanda balanced a cup of coffee in one hand and her notes and a map of New Orleans on her lap as she maneuvered the rented Buick through the French Quarter. A light rain was falling, cleaning the dirt and grime off the streets. She braked for a light as she watched tourists huddled under umbrellas, making their way from cafés and shops. Ellie LeBeaux, who had claimed to see an angel, sounded perfectly normal on the phone. In fact, Amanda could even say she sounded gracious. Still, you never know about people, so she was prepared for anything. Especially when Ellie gave her directions to her home and told Amanda that she lived on St. Peter Street, just off of the Quarter.

A horn beeped behind her. Amanda glanced back at the driver through her mirror and then noticed that the light had turned green. She accelerated and quickly glanced down at her notes. Ellie said she lived at the end of St. Peter Street by Jackson Square. Just past Canal was Royal, where she needed to turn left, then a quick right on St. Peter. She checked her notes again for the number: 441. As she pulled up to the building, she was lucky to find a parking spot in front of the beige three-story building. Black wrought-iron balconies adorned each story, and black shutters framed the building.

"Three-zero-six," Amanda said aloud as she checked her notes one more time. Ellie told her it was a three-story walkup. She stashed her tape recorder in her purse, locked her car, and began climbing the stairs. Slightly out of breath, Amanda finally reached the door and knocked softly. A moment later, the door opened only six inches, revealing a slightly heavyset, gray-haired black woman.

"Yes?" she asked hesitantly.

"Mrs. LeBeaux?"

"Yes," she said again.

"I'm Amanda Fox with WNN. We spoke yesterday morning."

Ellie LeBeaux smiled. "Yes, of course," she said as she opened the door. The mouthwatering aroma of freshly baked cookies permeated the air. "Please come in." She led her into the tiny studio apartment and said, "I have cookies just out of the oven. Please have a seat at the table and I'll bring them over. Would you like a cup of tea?"

"Yes, thank you," Amanda said.

As Ellie put the teakettle on, Amanda glanced around the small, comfortably furnished room. A small silver cross hung by the front door. Several magazines sat neatly displayed on the coffee table in front of the sofa. Behind the sofa, another table held a lamp and what appeared to be a multitude of family pictures. Moments later, Ellie brought in a plate of warm macaroons and a steaming pot of tea.

"Mrs. LeBeaux," Amanda said, "thank you for seeing me today."

"Please call me Ellie." She smiled as she poured. "Everybody does."

Amanda returned the smile. "Ellie, would you mind if I record our interview today? It helps me to be accurate in what I report."

"That would be fine."

Amanda spoke slowly, matching Ellie's pace. "You have reported seeing an angel. Can you tell me where this happened?"

"Yes. It was at the cemetery."

Amanda hesitated for a moment. "When was this?"

Ellie stopped for a moment. "It was on Monday. I know that because every Monday I visit my Reginald and my babies at the Lafayette Cemetery." She paused. "Reginald was my husband, and since he passed, there's not a Monday that's gone by that I haven't been there. But this Monday was different."

"What do you mean?"

"I don't know. It just felt different. I took the St. Charles streetcar, as I always do. I usually go in the morning when it's already crowded, but that Monday morning, it was unusually quiet. I told Reginald and my babies that I missed them, and I gave them carnations and macaroons. Oh, Reginald loves my macaroons." Ellie noticed the surprised look on Amanda's face and smiled, "Oh, I know the birds eat them, but I think my Reginald knows I bring them for him. Anyway, after I said goodbye, and left, I heard someone call my name. Well, I looked around and thought surely I must be hearing things. And then I heard it again, 'Ellie.' I looked over and saw a man sitting on a tomb."

"Excuse me," Amanda said. "This was a man?"

"Yes, and he said, "Ellie, don't be afraid.""

She stopped for a moment and then looked deeply into Amanda's eyes. "And then he said, 'God loves you and has chosen you to deliver a message. Tell them that the Lord, your God, has loved His people, but they have not loved Him. Tell them that the Lord wants His people to prepare themselves.' "

Amanda was momentarily speechless, but quickly regained her composure. "And then what happened?"

"He smiled and stroked my cheek with the back of this finger." She put her hand on her face. "I can still feel it."

"Did he say anything else?"

"No. He just left."

"Left how? Did he fly? Did he have wings?"

"Yes, he had wings, but no," Ellie said softly. "He just...," her voice trailed off.

"What?"

"He just disappeared."

There was a stunned silence for a moment. Finally, Amanda said, "That's an amazing story. You must have been very frightened."

"No, not frightened. I don't know why they chose me, but I feel very blessed. God has plans for all of us. This is mine. I've had many discussions with Pastor Thomas about it."

"Pastor Thomas?"

"Yes. He's the minister at our church."

"Which church is that?"

"Bethany Baptist. I've been a member for seventy-four years."

"Good heavens. That's a long time."

Ellie laughed, "Yes, it is. I was baptized there, was married there, and raised my children there."

"Do your children live close by?"

"Oh, yes. All five of them." She momentarily looked toward the photos on the table and smiled. "I had seven, but I lost two of my babies. One was just a year-and-a-half when she passed from scarlet fever. My oldest son, Reginald Jr., joined his sister when he was twenty- eight. He was a lieutenant in the army. He died in Vietnam. They're both buried next to Reginald at the Lafayette Cemetery."

"I'm so sorry," Amanda said.

"Thank you," Ellie said. She pushed herself from the table and stood. "May I get you some more tea?"

"No," Amanda said softly. "No, but thank you." Amanda stood and extended her hand. "Thank you for taking the time to talk with me."

Ellie smiled as she clasped Amanda's hand. "That's all right."

As Amanda looked into Ellie's gentle eyes, a thought came to her. "Ellie, would it be possible to interview you on camera?"

Ellie shook her head and laughed. "Oh, I don't know that I could do that."

"It really would be fairly painless. Just tell me once again exactly what you just told me." Amanda realized she was pushing a little too hard and forced herself to slow down. "Ellie," Amanda said softly, "If the angel told you that you were chosen to deliver a message to the world, this interview would reach many people. Would you at least think about it?"

Ellie nodded. "I'll pray about it."

Amanda took out a business card and wrote her cell number on the back. "Call me. I'll be in town for another couple of days."

A few moments later, Amanda was back in the car heading north on St. Louis Street. She was more shaken than she cared to admit. Ellie was so clear in her descriptions and so frighteningly believable. She recalled reading somewhere that people with dementia can sometimes be very believable. Then again, if Ellie were schizophrenic, perhaps she could believe with all her heart that her other personality saw the angel. What other possibility could there be?

Her mind was going at light speed when she remembered Ellie mentioning that she told her minister about the sighting. What was that church? Bethany something, she thought. Reaching for her cell phone, she searched for Bethany Church in New Orleans. Bethany Baptist. Yes, that was it, she thought as she punched in the number. The call was immediately connected, and she heard the phone ringing.

"Good morning. Bethany Baptist."

"Hello. My name is Amanda Fox. I'm a reporter with WNN News. Is Pastor Thomas there by any chance?"

A moment later, a deep baritone voice came on the line. "Hello, this is Pastor Thomas."

"Oh, hello Pastor. My name is Amanda Fox. I'm a reporter at WNN. I hope I'm not catching you at a bad time, but I was wondering if it would be possible to meet with you sometime today if your schedule would allow it. Well, yes, I'm in the Quarter now." She hesitated a moment as she listened. "The corner of Chartles and Toulouse? Okay. I'll see you shortly." Amanda glanced at her map. She was only a block away.

As soon as she turned left on Chartles, the large brick church came into view. She parked in the lot out front and pulled open the heavy door. The musty, sweet smell of polished woods and ancient hymnals immediately reminded her of St. Theresa's in Portland, Oregon, the Catholic Church she and her family attended when she was young. As Amanda entered, she saw a young lady in the outer office busy collating church programs. The name-plate on the desk said Mary Beth Hodges, Church Secretary.

"Good morning," she said. "May I help you?"

"Good morning," replied Amanda. "I'm Amanda Fox with WNN News. I just spoke to Pastor Thomas, and he's expecting me."

"Yes," she said and gave Amanda a warm smile. "Pastor Thomas told me. He's on the phone at the moment, but he shouldn't be long. I'm afraid there's not a lot of room around here to sit, but can I get you a cup of coffee while you're waiting?"

"Oh, thanks, but no, I just had tea." Amanda looked around at all the bulletins. "It looks like you've got your hands full."

"Umm," she agreed. "We're a large church with three services. This is only half the bulletins." The door to the inner office opened, revealing a tall man wearing a black shirt under his black suit. His slightly gray hair contrasted sharply with his youthful face. "Pastor," Mary Beth said, "this is Amanda Fox with WNN."

He extended his hand. "James Thomas," he said as he shook Amanda's hand. "Nice to meet you. Please, come in." The small office that held a large desk and chair plus two smaller chairs was made even smaller by the floor to ceiling bookcases that spanned the wall behind his desk. "Please, sit down," he said as he took a seat in his large, well-worn burgundy leather chair. "How can I help you?"

"First, thank you for seeing me today. I just left Ellie LeBeaux. She was kind enough to talk to me about her angel sighting."

Pastor Thomas clasped his hands in front of him and smiled. "And you were wondering if she's crazy."

Amanda laughed, "Well, maybe not crazy, but I just wondered what you knew about her. She said she's been a member here for seventy-four years."

"That's right. Much longer than I have. Miss Ellie's an institution around here."

"She said she told you about the angel sighting."

"Yes, she did," he said matter-of-factly.

"I have to say she told quite a fantastic story," Amanda said as she carefully watched the minister for his reaction. "Pastor Thomas, since you know Ellie so well, would you ever say that she sometimes might embellish the truth?"

He smiled. "Never."

"So you believe her?"

"Ms. Fox, faith is believing when you haven't seen it yourself. Yes, I believe her. The good Lord knew just what he was doing when he chose Miss Ellie to deliver his message. There isn't a finer woman around."

Amanda looked into his eyes questioningly. "So, do you think the end time is now?"

"I think, Ms. Fox, we're overdue."

Amanda set her tape recorder on the bed as she walked into her room at the Marriott and looked out the rain-streaked window to the city scene below. Her thoughts drifted back to Ellie and the interview. She just seemed so believable, she thought. Why would she make something like this up? Why would a minister be defending her? Were they looking for publicity for the church? She went back to the bed, sat down, and replayed the interview one more time.

"Hi April, it's Amanda. Is Mark around?" A moment later, Mark came on the line.

"Hi. Saw the piece on the abortion clinic bombing. Good job," he said. "Are you going to do any follow-ups?"

"No, I don't think so. It's pretty much an open and shut case since the bomber not only killed himself but left a confession behind. Such a waste."

"I know," Mark said quietly.

"After I left the clinic, I called Ellie LeBeaux, the lady who said she saw an angel, and asked if I could see her. I just got back."

"Did Pete go with you?"

"No, I didn't want to intimidate her with two people and a camera. She seemed so shy on the phone."

"So, what do you think? Is she a little off-kilter?"

"If she is, she hides it really well. I'm not even sure what to think, Mark. She was so believable it was frightening. I've got it all on tape."

"So, what happened?"

"Better that you hear it yourself," Amanda said as she rewound the recorder and hit play.

"Wow," Mark whispered after the interview had finished.

"Yeah," Amanda said. "I was pretty blown away. She mentioned her minister, so I went to see him.

"What did he say?

"He said he's known her forever, and he absolutely believes her. I don't know, maybe they're trying to cook something up for publicity. I asked her if she would go on camera. Pete's still here to tape it."

"Careful, Amanda. Are you sure this is the story you want to report?"

"I don't know. I just have a gut feeling about it. She's not even sure she wants to do it. She said she'd pray about it." Amanda was quiet for a moment. "It's just such a coincidence with that Greek lady in Rome. I mean, two people coming up with the same kind of story."

"Well, good luck. Just keep in touch."

She clicked off her phone and walked over to the sink, grabbed a freshly folded washcloth, ran it under cold water, then held it against the nape of her neck. The coolness melted the tension away. She took a deep breath and set the cloth on the sink when she heard her cell phone. Picking it up, she saw it was Ellie. She touched the screen. "Amanda Fox."

"Ms. Fox? This is Ellie LeBeaux. I've been thinking about what you said about how being interviewed would help spread God's message, so if you still want me to go on camera, I will."

CHAPTER FIVE

R everend John sat at the desk in his study and scanned through the contacts on his computer, jotting down names and numbers. Fund-raising was a necessary evil when you ran a five-hundred-million-dollar empire. In a perverse way, though, it was almost an enjoyable task. Mostly because over two hundred million had been siphoned into his own personal offshore account, which supported homes in Aspen, Scottsdale, and La Jolla, as well as an eighty-foot yacht tied up in the Cayman Islands.

Additionally, this little nest egg paid for a Gulfstream jet, which was conveniently hidden in a secluded hangar at the Baton Rouge Municipal Airport. Outwardly though, he lived in a modest $250,000 home in Baton Rouge, where he entertained parishioners and corporate leaders. The other homes, the jet, and his yacht were all listed under various aliases, purchased with funds from a Swiss bank account. He learned this trick when he was a young minister. Frank Bennelli, a member of his church who just happened to have ties to the Mafia, taught him about fund-raising and how to hide information from the IRS, presumably to help Reverend John keep more money to build his church.

Unfortunately, Frank had met an early demise. They found him shot to death in his home. However, the lessons that he taught Reverend John lived on and, through the years, the good reverend embellished those lessons with a few thoughts of his own. He recently had come across a real estate deal in Boca Raton that was too good to pass up, but he was several million short. So, it was time to raise funds again. As he was looking through the names, he stopped at C.J. Kemper, head of Kemper Health.

According to the Wall Street Journal, Kemper had just acquired Rutherford Health, making Kemper the largest health care provider in America. He and C.J. were members of the board of directors of Myernet and, although C.J. wasn't a member of Reverend John's church, he had been generous from time to time when Reverend John had called on him for charity. He picked up his phone, punched in C.J.'s private number, and cleared his throat. "C.J.," Reverend John boomed. "This is Reverend John. I hope I'm not catching you at a bad time."

"Not at all," C.J. replied warmly. "How are you, John?"

Being called John, instead of Reverend John, slightly irritated him, but focusing on the estate in Boca Raton, he hid it well. "Fine. I'm just fine, although I have to admit, I'm calling you for a favor. As you know, we've been building a children's wing on to Mercy Hospital. It's just so important since so many of these little tykes have not had the care that they've needed. Once this wing is finished, Mercy will have the finest children's health care facility in the country. But, of course, nothing is free these days. I was wondering if I might put you down for a donation."

"How much do you need?"

"Well, we're looking at about three and a half million to finish the project right. Now, I certainly don't expect you to contribute that kind of money, but any type of donation would be appreciated. I've been praying about it, and I know that the good Lord will lead me to others like yourself who will help this worthy cause."

"You've caught me at a good time, John. I believe in this project just as much as you do, maybe even more, since I lost my son to cancer." He was quiet for a moment. "It was such a long time ago, but it seems like yesterday. You'll have your money. I'll get a check out to you today."

"God in all his mercy will bless you, C.J. Thank you. Thank you so much."

"If I can help other children, that's all the thanks I need."

Reverend John set the phone down and momentarily felt a twinge of guilt but banished it quickly. It was true that the Spirit of Truth Church was building a children's wing on to Mercy Hospital, so he didn't lie. Not entirely anyway. The money, however, had been in place a long time ago through the generosity of his television audience, but if C.J. wanted to believe that he was responsible for completing the children's wing, so much the better. The wing would be completed, C.J. would feel good about himself, and he would have his new estate in Boca. Everybody wins, he thought, as he sat back and clasped his hands over his stomach. God is good.

He got up from his desk, retrieved a bottle of cognac from the armoire, poured himself a drink and nestled into a large brown leather chair just in time to catch the five o'clock news. At 5:50, he became bored and began flipping through the channels. When he reached "The Week-End Report with Amanda Fox" he thought he recognized the man on camera.

"So, Pastor Thomas," Amanda said, "Ellie LeBeaux is a member of your church?"

Well, lookie there, thought Reverend John. James Thomas. It's been a long time. In fact, it had been over twenty-three years since he had last seen him, but he remembered Thomas very clearly. That sniveling little do-gooder was part of a group that was responsible for him losing the license for his first television station. "Lack of moral turpitude" the FCC had called it, with claims of shady financial dealings. Nothing could really be proven, but when the government traced the ownership of the station to Reverend John's friend, who had ties to illegal gambling, the license was revoked and his station was closed. But Reverend John was only temporarily out of business. He soon found a home on cable which, thank heavens, allowed almost anything.

"We actually have Ellie's description of the angel encounter on tape and we'll let you, the studio audience, decide for yourself," Amanda said. Reverend John was transfixed as he watched the interview, momentarily forgetting his disgust of James Thomas.

"Thank you, Pastor Thomas, for being with us today," Amanda said, and then turned back toward the camera.

"We have to go to a quick break, but when we return, we'll have the latest on the search for nine-year-old Angela Taylor."

Reverend John clicked off the television as he thought about his old nemesis. Maybe the man was finally coming around, with his talk about angel sightings and end times. Oldest trick in the book, thought Reverend John. For as far back as he could remember, there had always been someone preaching about the end times. One old man in particular had stayed in his memory.

John was six at the time, and his mother had taken him to downtown Los Angeles to shop for shoes at Bullock's. On their way from the bus to the store, he saw a giant of a man with a long gray beard standing on a park bench yelling about repentance. Johnny didn't know what repentance meant, but he knew it was scary and he didn't want anything to do with it. Still, the man fascinated him.

As his mother hurried along, he let go of her hand and stood looking up at the preacher. The old man stopped for a moment, pointed at him, and told him he was not too young to think about his salvation. Then, a wonderful thing happened. He noticed that the old man's hat was turned upside down, and someone actually walked by and put a dollar in it. A dollar. Seconds later, his mother grabbed his hand and pulled him toward the store. But the memory of that man making money so easily was an epiphany.

John took another sip of cognac as an idea began to fester within him. Why should that pompous jerk and his penny-ante church get all the publicity? He was the believable one. He was Reverend John. He already had a huge following and people adored him. In fact, they'd believe almost anything he said. Why shouldn't he cash in? This angel thing could be big. Really big. He went to his desk, retrieved a yellow legal pad, and started making notes for his next sermon

CHAPTER SIX

A manda punched in the number for the fourth time in an hour and, as before, was only greeted with the constant ringing of the phone on the other end. She had been back from New Orleans for over a week, but the interview with Ellie LeBeaux still haunted her. Impossible as she knew the story was, there was just something so genuine about Ellie. She wanted answers and her journalistic instincts told her that the lady in Rome might hold some. She glanced at her watch—11:31 a.m. It would be 5:31 p.m. in Greece. The phone rang and rang. Thinking she may have misdialed, she dialed again, but with the same results.

Frustrated, she walked down the hall to the new cappuccino machine. What management deemed as a perk, Amanda strongly suspected was more a ploy to keep the staff wired and alert 24/7. She saw that Dave Markham, the anchor for the six o'clock news, was already there with the same idea in mind.

"Morning, Amanda," he said, stirring whipped cream into his coffee. "By the way, good interview with the lady from New Orleans. Think there's anything to it?"

"I don't know," she said as she flicked the machine on. "All we can do is report it. I'll tell you, though, she sure seemed honest."

"Well, if the end of the world is coming, let me know," he said with a laugh as he turned to leave. "See you later."

As she watched the coffee slowly drizzle into the cup, she thought about Dave's flippant remark. Maybe he's right, she thought. Maybe I'm taking this too seriously. As much as she wanted it, she decided to forgo the whipped cream.

She took the coffee back to her office and dialed the number in Greece one more time.

"Kalispera," a man's voice said rapidly.

"Kalispera," Amanda said haltingly. "Good evening. Is this the residence of Anna Kraikos?"

"Yes, who is this?"

"I'm sorry, this is Amanda Fox. I'm a reporter with WNN and I met Anna in Rome. She asked me to come to Greece to speak to her brother. Is she at home?"

"No," the man replied brusquely.

"Well, can you tell me when it might be best to reach her?"

"I don't know what time my wife will return."

Despite his rudeness, Amanda's voice remained calm. "Mr. Kraikos, Anna asked me to come to Kalymnos to speak to Niko about his angel sighting and…"

"Oh, that," he said, cutting her off. "Niko's sometimes crazy when he drinks too much. My wife, she worries about him."

"So you're saying he didn't see an angel?"

"No," he said forcefully. "No angel. Look, I'm hanging up now."

"Would you at least tell Anna that I called?"

"Yeah, sure," he blurted.

"And, Mr. Kraikos, would you tell Niko that he's not the only one who has seen an angel?" There was silence on the other end of the phone. "Mr. Kraikos?"

"Yeah, I heard you," he said quietly. "Andio." The line went dead.

She was deep in thought and didn't notice that Mark had come in. "Amanda?"

30

Startled, she looked up at him. He gave her a smile. "Good morning," she said, straightening up and taking a breath. "I just got off the phone with Anna Kraikos' husband in Greece."

"Anna Kraikos?" he asked with a slight shrug.

"Remember, the lady in Rome I told you about who said her brother had seen the angel? That was Anna Kraikos. She wasn't there, but her husband was, and I tell you he couldn't wait to get me off the phone. He said that the brother had been drinking, and apparently made up the whole thing." She sat back in her chair and held her coffee between her hands. "So either he's lying or Ellie is or, who knows, maybe they're in this together. Or maybe I'm just trying to make something out of nothing."

"You'll have another chance to find out," he said as he handed her a news wire. She put her coffee on the desk as she scanned the wire. "Lima, Peru. Accused robber, Manuel Guzman, 39, became violent and was rushed to infirmary after claims of seeing an angel in his prison cell."

She looked up at Mark. "Another one?"

Mark nodded. "I'd say it was a copy-cat, but the guy was in prison. In fact, he still is."

"Yeah, well, he could have had a visitor who told him about Ellie." She shrugged. "Maybe, he thought the infirmary would be better than his cell."

"Maybe," Mark replied.

"You know I've got to go talk to him," she said with a faint smile.

Mark returned the smile. "I know. You and Vargas are booked on a flight tomorrow morning."

Amanda laughed. "Whether I want to or not, huh?"

"As if anyone could keep you away."

Amanda sat back and took a sip of her coffee. "What do you really think is going on, Mark?"

"No idea," he said as his expression stilled. "But I do know that whatever the truth is, you'll find it. Just keep in touch and watch your step. It can be tricky down there."

She smiled. "Thanks, I will."

CHAPTER SEVEN

The desert night was clear and cold as George Wilson adjusted his telescope for the third time that evening. The new target was in the Scorpios constellation, focusing on M6, known as the Butterfly Cluster, which was directly off the tip of the scorpion's tail. Normally, this was a lonely vigil, but tonight his friend and fellow airline pilot and amateur astronomer Jim Montemayor had joined him with his homemade Newtonian telescope for viewing M70 in the Sagittarius constellation - the same constellation in which Tom Bopp first sighted the Hale-Bopp comet. They each worked in silence as they studied the heavens and periodically checked their charts. A chilly Arizona wind rippled across Bartlett Lake, disturbing their equipment.

"I don't know how much longer we can stay out here if this wind keeps up," said Jim as he zipped up his jacket in deference to the cold.

"Let's give it a little longer," said George, refocusing his telescope. As he panned across the sky toward M70 a small blur caught his eye. He cleaned the lens and looked again. The blur was still there. He quickly checked his charts and saw no mention of a star in that quadrant. "Jim, come here. Look at this," he said. As Jim peered through the telescope, George noted the time and position of the blur in his notebook.

"What do you mean? The star?"

"That's no star," said George, "At least it's not on the chart. I'll bet it's a comet."

"Wow," Jim said as he continued watching it.

"We'll know in an hour if it's changed positions."

Excitement was beginning to build as the time passed. They noticed that not only was the object moving to the east, but it seemed to become more intense. "We need to get this information to the Central Bureau," said George as he jotted the new position in his notebook. "Maybe we'll have another Hale-Bopp, or at least a Kohoutek."

"Or a Wilson," Jim said with a broad smile.

CHAPTER EIGHT

The Boeing 757 made its final turbulent descent through the heavy cloud cover, bounced twice then touched down at Jorge Chavez International Airport. Amanda checked her watch: 6:35 p.m.—twenty minutes late. Outside the windows, only fog-shrouded gray buildings could be seen as they taxied to the gate.

"Well, we're here," she said to her cameraman as she unbuckled her seat belt. Fifteen minutes later, they had finally deplaned and followed the long line of tired travelers through the dimly lit corridors of the customs hall. A silent, sullen agent examined their passports, his eyes sharply assessing their faces. Satisfied, he added a Peru stamp on each passport and shoved them back. Another agent examined their luggage; closely studying Pete's battle-scarred Sony Betacam. Seeing no black-market value in the oversized camera, he decided not to confiscate it and waved them through to the exit.

"Let's find a cab," Amanda said as she pulled her carry-on behind her. Outside, the cool evening air was pungent with the smoke of cooking fires mixed with the unmuffled exhaust of ancient diesel buses on the highway into Lima. The crowd shouted to the new arrivals, offering food, drink, Chiclets, cigarettes, and taxi services. Amanda and Pete picked the only taxi driver shouting in English, loaded their luggage and equipment, and said a silent prayer as the battered Toyota eased into the rush-hour traffic.

Nearing the Embassy District, the roads narrowed to little more than two-lane alleys. They wound past tidy white stucco town-homes, each secured with locked gates and high, broken glass-topped walls. They passed the old Catholic girl's school which was quiet at this hour. Earlier in the day, traffic often came to a stop as brand-new Mercedes limousines lined up at the entrance, waiting to unload the daughters of government officials, high-ranking military officers, bankers, arms traders, and other privileged classes. Finally, the taxi pulled up to the curb in front of the Swiss Hotel, and Amanda and Pete entered through the twelve-foot-tall glass doors into an enormous marble-lined lobby with a sweeping, gold-railed staircase.

"Man," said Pete as he looked up at the crystal chandeliers that hung from the twenty-foot ceiling.

"Glitz for the tourists," Amanda replied as she made her way to the reservation desk. "Let's get our rooms and unload. I don't know about you, but I'm starving. Our choices here are Italian or Swiss."

"Italian," Pete said quickly.

Thirty minutes later, Amanda was sipping a glass of rich, red Solyss wine and Pete was enjoying a beer as they waited for dinner.

"Any plans yet on how we're going to get into the jail?"

"I'm working on Plan C now," Amanda said.

"Plan C? What happened to A and B?"

Amanda waved her hand. "Not important. Either one of them would probably have landed us in jail. Anyway, it's not going to be 'us.' I'm going in by myself."

"Uh, that could be tricky."

"Look, you know they're not going to let reporters in. The only chance we've got is to tell them that I'm his sister-in-law from America and that I've got a message for him from his brother."

"I don't know. I have a bad feeling. What if they check?"

"Check what? I'll be in and out before they even have a chance to check."

"You're going to have to speak to them somehow. Do you even speak Spanish?"

"Si, fluently. Almost. Two years of high school and four years of college Spanish and I've had lots of practice in the meantime. It'll come back," she said simply. "That's the least of my problems. I need to go shopping first. I'm way overdressed and I need some men's clothes."

The next morning Amanda, dressed simply in a white blouse and a long blue skirt, could have easily passed for a local—especially now that her auburn hair was tucked into a black wig. Two men's shirts and a pair of pants were loosely wrapped in brown paper and tucked under her arm."Okay, Amanda. Forty-five minutes. If I don't hear from you, I'm calling Mark and the American Embassy."

"Don't worry," she said. "I'll be fine." As she walked up the steps to the entrance, two policemen holding a prisoner between them shoved her out of the way, almost knocking her off her feet. She took a deep breath and continued on to the door that had just slammed in front of her. As she tentatively entered the room, she heard shouting.

The prisoner was trying to explain something to the man behind the counter, but was told to shut up and sit down. When the prisoner kept trying to explain, one of the police officers hit him and shoved him into a chair. As the commotion died down, the man behind the desk noticed Amanda. The others followed his gaze and soon all eyes were on her.

"Que usted desea?" What do you want?

"Please, sir," Amanda said in faltering Spanish, "I would like to see one of your prisoners for just a moment. It's my brother-in-law, Manuel Guzman. My husband and I live in America and his brother is very ill. We have just heard that Manuel is in prison and my husband has asked me to see him and bring some clean clothes."

"Póngalos en el contador. Le los daremos. Put them on the counter. We'll give them to him."

"That's very kind of you. My husband will be very happy." She carefully placed the clothes on the counter. "He also had a message for him. It's about his mother. She's going in for a gall bladder operation in three weeks. The name of the hospital is—"

"Enough," the commandant said, shoving the clothes to the floor. "Tell him yourself." He signaled the guard. "Let her in."

"Oh, thank you," Amanda said as she gathered the clothes from the ground. "You are a kind man." She heard laughter behind her as she was led down the dark hallway to a row of cells. The guard stopped and opened the second to the last one on the left.

"Five minutes," he said, slamming the door behind her.

The sunken eyes and hollowed cheeks of the prisoner showed serious health problems. Amanda had seen the look before when she was a journalism student at the University of Iowa. One of her assignments was to cover the street people in Des Moines, many with major drug and malnutrition problems. She had come to know too well the look of impending death. "Senor Guzman?"

The man eyed her suspiciously. "Quienes son usted?" Who are you?

"My name is Amanda," she began slowly. "Do you speak English?" He nodded slightly as he kept his eyes on her. "I know about the angels."

He narrowed his eyes. "Who told you?" he urgently whispered.

"Senor Guzman, I am a reporter with WNN, an American news network. You're not the only one who has seen the angels. There have been others."

His eyes opened wide. "There have been others? They told me I was crazy. They told me I was out of my head."

"Can you tell me what happened?" Amanda asked gently.

He looked at her without speaking. Finally, he said quietly "It was here. I was sleeping. I heard someone call me. 'Manny,' she said. I was sleeping, you see, and when I heard this voice, I turned over and saw a woman." Tears began to well in his eyes. "She called my name again, said that God loves me and has chosen me to bring a message to the world." He stopped and took a breath.

"What was the message?"

He looked at her and said, "She said that God wanted me to tell them that God has loved His people, but they have not loved Him." He stopped and began to sob softly. He continued brokenly, "And then she said to tell God's people to prepare themselves."

"Did anything else happen?"

"Yes," he said, tears streaming down his face. "She said again that God loves me and then she stroked my cheek with the back of her finger and then…"

"She left?"

Manny looked down. "She disappeared."

"I know," Amanda said quietly.

"Five minutes are up," the guard said loudly as he unlocked the cell door.

"These are for you," Amanda said as she handed him the clothes. "Thank you, Manny. Take good care."

Pete watched her quickly coming toward him. "Well, you made it back in one piece and no one's chasing you, Amanda. So, did you see him?"

Yeah," she whispered as she looked back toward the jail. Something's going on here, Pete. Either this is the biggest hoax the world has ever known, or Armageddon really is coming."

CHAPTER NINE

The last flight back to the U.S. left at 12:35 a.m. Amanda and Pete were on it. Pete fell asleep immediately, but Amanda could only stare out at the empty blackness. She kept seeing the faces of Ellie and Manny as they told her about the sightings. Logic told her this couldn't be real, yet both of them seemed so believable. What if this was a hoax? Could these people be connected? Why would they do this? She grabbed her pillow and cradled her head against the window, but the images kept haunting her. Could this be real? What if it really is a message from God? She involuntarily shuddered and pulled a blanket around her.

At 11:42 a.m. they touched down at Dulles and taxied to the gate. Amanda immediately turned on her cell phone and saw that she had four voice mails. She pulled out her phone and plugged one ear as she tried to block out the young lady behind her, who had not stopped talking for the last three hours. Quickly making notes, she punched in each new message.

"Oh, no," she said as she listened.

Pete turned quickly, "What?"

"They found Angela, the little girl who was missing. They found her in a trash dumpster. She was nude."

"What's the matter with people?" Pete asked.

Amanda shook her head in frustration. "I don't know."

The passengers had deplaned ahead of them and the young lady who had been so conversational waited for them as they grabbed their bags and joined the line out the door.

As she made her way down the aisle, Amanda said over her shoulder, "I hope the customs line isn't long. I need to get back to the studio, but I'm going home first."

It was just after one o'clock when Amanda finally walked through her front door. The small, neat, one-bedroom apartment was furnished with oversized, comfortable furniture and some antiques she had found when she moved to D.C. She deposited her bag on the queen-sized sleigh bed, went into the kitchen, and grabbed a diet coke from the refrigerator and poured it into a wine glass. She heard her phone ring and quickly retrieved it from her purse. Checking caller id, a momentary surge of guilt hit Amanda. It had been a while since she talked with her father.

Amanda clicked the phone on. "Hey, Dad."

Her father's deep, resonant voice came on the line. "How are you?"

"I'm fine. There's just a lot going on right now."

"I know. I've been watching the news and saw your report on the angel sighting."

"Yeah, it has been pretty amazing."

"So, what's my number one skeptic think of all this?"

"To be honest, I don't know," she said, slightly irritated at her father's question. Skeptic was a favorite word of his when it came to Amanda. "There was actually a second sighting," she continued. "I just got in from Peru. Both of these people seem genuine, but it's still a little hard to believe." After an awkward silence, Amanda said, "Dad, I'm sorry, but I've got to get going. I need to get back to the studio this afternoon to tie some things up."

"I understand. Just wanted to touch base. I love you, Amanda."

Amanda hesitated, then said quietly, "Love you, too."

Her relationship with her father had always been strained, due in no small part to their differing views of religion. As a devout Catholic, there were certain expectations to be met, and he never wavered on them. He expected his family to be at church every Sunday. He expected everyone's faithful attendance at confession, which Amanda hated with a passion.

The Ten Commandments were not ten suggestions, as he often said, they were commandments. There was no gray with him. It was simply black and white. Unfair as it might be, she always felt somehow that God Himself had a hand in her misery. While she rebelled, her brother David did just the opposite and became closer and closer to the church. When he finally became a priest, she had cried.

CHAPTER TEN

"Praise the Lord," Reverend John shouted to his congregation. "Praise the Lord. God is alive and has sent me a wondrous miracle. A miracle so great that I want to shout it from the rooftops but, at the same time, this miracle has left me so very humbled. While I was in prayer two days ago, I had a vision of a beautiful angel who was calling to me and when I opened my eyes, she was actually standing there in front of me. "She was real and she was gul-lor-ious with her long flowing yellow hair and white gown. I was so overcome by the power of God above that I fell to my knees." He took a moment and dabbed his eyes with a handkerchief. "She told me not to be afraid," he continued, "and that she was sent to me to deliver a message."

Several "hallelujahs" and a loud "praise be" could be heard in the congregation.

"She said God is pleased with the Spirit of Truth Church and with our ministry," he began, heavily emphasizing the word God. At this point his voice broke and Reverend John took a moment to regain himself. "This wonderful angel said that God wants a temple to be built to His honor—a temple larger than any on earth—so that He will know that we love Him. I wept and told her that I would do anything for

God. Then she smiled at me. Brothers and sisters, that smile was the most beautiful I have ever seen.

"And then," he continued, "she spread her wings, and I watched her fly back to heaven."

"Praise the Lord," someone shouted.

"I've been in seclusion for the last two days praying for guidance and help, and in praying about this, I believe with all my heart that God has chosen the Spirit of Truth Church because of all of you wonderful people." Applause broke out in the huge church. Reverend John continued, "I believe that God himself has sent you as partners in this wonderful mission." Ushers and prayer leaders stood up and led everyone else in a standing ovation. This time the applause lasted for several minutes.

Reverend John smiled and raised his hands to quiet the crowd. "Good people, we are all children of the Most High and we will together build His temple to all of His gul-lor-ry. This morning we are going to have a special offering to God—to His holy temple. Let us pray." All heads bowed as Reverend John paused a moment for dramatic effect. "Oh, Heavenly Father, we are but mere servants in your house. I pray that you open the hearts of all who hear me now. I pray that we put our total trust in you and know that all we give to you will be returned to us ten-fold as you have always promised. You have given us a great mission and we will not fail you. We come with our tithes and offerings with a loving heart. Please give blessings on each and every one who are willing, to show you their love by their generous gifts. Amen and amen."

On cue, the choir broke out in "How Great Thou Art." Reverend John then took a seat in full view of his congregation and leaned forward in prayer, dabbing his eyes occasionally with his handkerchief. As the ushers passed the plates, the television cameras panned the congregation and zoomed in on some of the members singing as tears rolled down their cheeks.

Benny McDuff occasionally glanced at the television and smiled as he made entries in his ledger. Even though it was Sunday, Benny was hard at work at his desk in the basement of the church. As chief financial officer of the Spirit of Truth Ministries, he found that Sunday was the opportune time to take care of certain matters that went beyond the church. He had been working for Reverend John since the early days when the good reverend first began his ministry. Frank Bennilli had actually introduced them while Benny was still in prison for embezzlement. Frank advised Reverend John to hire Benny as soon as he got out because, as Frank used to say, "The man's got a brain. He'll help you."

Benny not only had a brain, he was, in fact, a genius when it came to counting, multiplying, and laundering money. He was well paid with five percent of the take after expenses. Reverend John knew Benny would never expose him, because the money was just too good. They laughingly deemed their relationship an "unholy alliance."

Benny watched as Reverend John said his final prayer and the spokesman for the church came on with his appeal to join the Spirit of Truth Fellowship.

"For only $395 per year," the spokesman said, "you'll all have the sermons, outlines, and notes used by Reverend John in his weekly broadcast. You can attend the conferences and spiritually renewing crusades free of charge. You'll have special seating in the services and conferences—front row seats, specially lit for the cameras. Many in our congregation have become celebrities in their own right. Finally, you'll get a ten percent discount on all Spirit of Truth books, CDs, DVDs, and videos."

Recently, Benny came up with the idea of offering life and health insurance to members at a twenty percent discount, and the Truth Insurance Company was born. This was one of the best ideas he ever had, because the money was flowing in—then disappearing into numerous offshore accounts, earning tax-free interest, hidden forever from the IRS.

Benny picked up C.J. Kemper's $3,500,000 check. After posting it in the private ledger, he put it aside to ask Reverend John where he wanted the money filtered. He looked up when he heard the outer office door open. Reverend John came in, slowly lowered his enormous bulk into a chair and loosened his tie. "So," he asked as a smile flashed across his face, "was I believable?"

"Oscar worthy," Benny replied as he sat back in his chair.

"What do you think, money-wise?"

"I'd say between the extra offerings, the television donations and the increased memberships in the Spirit of Truth Fellowship, we're probably looking at another hundred million a year, maybe more. Of course, when you add in the Truth Insurance premiums, I'd say you could double that. We can probably milk the temple thing for at least a year or two."

Reverend John frowned. "Well, we can't just milk it, Benny. We actually have to build something. It's time for a new church anyway, something worthy of the Spirit of Truth Ministries—a magnificent shrine. Something the people can look at and say that they built it." His expression changed to a sly grin. "But, you know, we can raise the hundred million a year that you say we will, but I'll bet we'll be able to build it for half that cost." He let out a contented sigh. "It's all working out, isn't it Benny?"

Benny just nodded and chuckled.

CHAPTER ELEVEN

At the Keck Observatory's remote offices in Waimea, Hawaii, a team of scientists and astronomers were being briefed on the new Wilson Comet. They were astounded by the news that chief astronomer Dr. Steven Hoshiwara was telling them.

"This comet is the largest ever recorded, measuring 250 kilometers at its nucleus. It was approximately one hundred fifty million miles from Earth when first discovered four days ago and, we have reason to believe that it originated from the Oort cloud. Due to the tremendous size of Comet Wilson, we have calculated the speed to be approximately forty miles per second. We believe that speed could conceivably pick up to sixty miles per second as it comes closer to Earth on its elliptical path. If we are correct, the comet will pass by us at a close three hundred thousand miles within the next six weeks. Although the path does not indicate a danger for Earth, the viewing by the naked eye will be nothing less than spectacular."

An astronomer from India, Dr. Alexander Bhutani spoke up. "Dr. Hoshiwara, would you tell us your opinion, given the size, if the gravitational pull of the earth could conceivably alter the path of this comet or in some way break it apart—not unlike the Shoemaker-Levy 9 Comet that broke into several pieces and collided with Jupiter?"

A more serious expression crossed Dr. Hoshiwara's face. "Yes, we have discussed that possibility. We feel, however, that due to its speed as it comes closer to Earth, the reverse should happen and the comet should be catapulted away from Earth. However, we have never dealt with a comet of this size before. Our calculations can only be based on prior experience and mathematical reasoning. As you know the gravitational pull of Jupiter is over two and a half times that of Earth."

"Understandably," Dr. Bhutani replied, "but the size of Shoemaker-Levy 9 was much smaller than this new comet. Given the size of the Wilson Comet, would that counter the weaker gravitational pull of Earth?"

"It's difficult to answer," replied Dr. Hoshiwara. "Our best calculations at the moment indicate that this comet will not come closer than three hundred thousand miles from Earth. We can all only hope these calculations are correct."

CHAPTER TWELVE

The sun momentarily peaked through gray clouds, then immediately retreated again—casting an ominous pall over the fifty-two acre estate. Armed guards were stationed in the guard house and at each point of entry to the thirty-five-thousand-square-foot mansion. Normally the secret group of twenty-seven, known as the Phoenix World Alliance, held their semi-annual meetings at undisclosed places in Europe.

This year, however, the Guardian tabloid had discovered the Paris location and the meeting was quickly rescheduled and moved to the New York home of Andrew J. Melton in the Hamptons. It was Andrew's grandfather, Horace R. Melton who began the group in 1912. Taking a Globalist approach to the unrest of the world just prior to World War I, he called together twenty-six of the world's elite, ostensibly to discuss politics. As the group continued to meet, discussions of politics turned to money and finally to control.

For most of the twentieth century, they actually controlled wars to their financial advantage. They decided when wars would start, how long they would last, who would win and who would receive the multi-billion dollar contracts for rebuilding. To protect themselves, they also had control of the media.

The majority of the world's news networks, and most of the major newspapers — as well as the major wire services and, most recently, certain influential internet blogs, were owned by them. Phoenix World Alliance thereby fed the public what they wanted the public to believe.

Today, the twenty-seven descendants of the original members also control the major financial institutions of the world. As a group, they decided international interest and exchange rates, the prices of gold and oil, and which countries received foreign aid grants and industrial aid loans. Payback is guaranteed: If the borrower makes good on their loans, they pocket the money; if the borrower defaults, the taxpayers who guarantee the loans are obligated to pay. Either way, the Alliance wins.

Their major control, however, has been in the political arena. The success of presidents, chancellors, and prime ministers are of their choosing. Unfortunately, so is the demise of politicians and other notables who either defy them or threatened to reveal them.

As the members sipped Hennessy Ellipse brandy in the enormous mahogany-lined library, Andrew Melton stood before the group holding a glass of Perrier. "Gentlemen," he began, "first let me welcome you to my home. It's not quite what we had in mind this year, but I trust you are comfortable." The others nodded and smiled. He stepped over and took a seat in a wing-backed leather chair and set his drink down on a side table.

"We have three items that need our immediate attention. The U.S. presidential election is coming up and decisions need to be made about who we will place in this very important position. Governor Paul Danover, I feel, is a strong candidate. Good looking, a good family man, and well liked. Another interesting possibility this year is Senator Darius Russell from California. She's a strong candidate and has had her eye on the presidency since she first entered politics. Certainly, they are both contenders. Discussion?"

"I have to agree with Danover," Lord Timothy Brighton ventured. "He's been a model governor since we first set him up in Rhode Island. Danover has stayed loyal to us and was especially helpful getting rid of his attorney general's call girl. He has certainly been flexible on anything we have asked of him, and I would think he would be the same way as president. I'm not so certain of the Russell woman. She's not well liked and has a reputation for double talk. She skates back and forth on every issue. I have to say, I don't quite trust her."

"Still," Ernesto Guirtierra added, flicking an ash from his cigar into the Waterford ashtray beside him. "Europe likes her. Perhaps even France might come around. This could be good financially."

"Perhaps," interjected Francois Montague, "but it may be hard to get the votes. In a word, gentlemen, she's dowdy. She may be strong, but definitely lacks any type of polish. "

"The least of our problems," Lord Brighton said. "Heaven knows, we've hired teams before to improve an image. I mean, take a look at some of the candidates in England. I, for one, thought many of those women were beyond hope, and yet they were made passable. No, my concern, as I said before, is the element of trust. Her ego, I believe, will be her downfall. I think once she gets into a position of power, she will quickly forget who put her there."

"I think we should speak to both of them and explain our expectations," Andrew said.

"Agreed," Lord Brighton said.

"Fine, then," said Andrew, "we will have our people schedule them for the next meeting in January." He took a sip of water. "The second item of business is this conflict between Israel and Iran. The situation is heating up to the point where Israel has said that Iran is prepared to use nuclear force against them. The Israeli president is pressuring the United States into joining forces with them, but with the U.S. having such a bad reputation throughout that part of the world as it is, I think this could be very much a mistake."

"I absolutely concur," Gioberto Meddici said. "If Israel wants to go to war, they should fight on their own."

"But, of course, if they do that," Lord Brighton said, "either they or Iran will face destruction. This could plunge us into World War III. No, I believe we need to quell this problem."

"The Israeli president is determined," Andrew said, "and I'm not positive he will back off so easily."

"Then," Gioberto said simply, "he may have to be eliminated." As each pondered the situation, the grandfather clock's slow, steady ticking was all that could be heard. Elimination was always such a messy business, but sometimes a necessary evil.

"Right, then," Lord Brighton said to no one in particular as he took a sip of Perrier. "I think we should give the chap one last chance. And if he doesn't respond properly, then we have no choice but to put our teams in place." The Alliance maintained teams of assassins, police officers, and medical teams in every country throughout the world. They would be instantly ready with one phone call. The medical teams were the most valuable because they were adept at covering up the cause of death.

"It might be wise to have a news release prewritten that details a heart attack caused by the tremendous stress the Israeli president has been under. I'll send it to our news outlets through discreet channels," Andrew said as he jotted a note and recapped his pen. "Now the last bit of business concerns this news about angel sightings." The others chuckled. "I know, but ridiculous as it is, people are getting nervous, and it's affecting the market. I think we can handle this by having our print and broadcast editors downplay these stories.

"It probably wouldn't hurt to go a step further and start discrediting some of these people," Gioberto said as he flicked an ash of his cigar into the crystal ashtray. "I don't think it's going to be too difficult, especially since some of them are of questionable character at best."

"I must say, I am surprised at Martin Scolesco at WNN for even allowing this diatribe to be reported, but he's always been a bit of a maverick," Andrew said. "I think WNN needs a little wake-up call. Perhaps pulling some of their sponsors might help them see the light of day. I would imagine our friends at the ACLU would be beneficial in this case, especially if we send some money their way. I'll call my people to get negative press out on this immediately."

"Be sure to include Hollywood," Lord Brighton added. "They'll have a field day with it." The others laughed.

Andrew Melton looked around the room. "Does anyone else have issues they would like to discuss?" Silence ensued and then he continued, "Fine, I'll remind you about our upcoming elections. We'll be meeting here once again in two weeks. As you know, this will be a three-day event, and we are providing accommodations here for you. Hopefully, the weather will cooperate, and we'll have some time to get some sailing in."

CHAPTER THIRTEEN

"Did you see this?" Mark asked as he tossed the New York Times on Amanda's desk. A front page above-the-fold story included a cartoon of an angel with fully extended wings holding the HNN microphone up to Amanda. The caption read, "Now really, isn't this just about the ratings?"

Amanda looked up at Mark with a wry smile. "HNN? What is that, the Hallelujah News Network?"

"I was thinking the Heaven News Network, but I like Hallelujah better."

She shook her head. "This is nothing compared to Jimmy last night."

"Missed it. What happened?"

"Nothing worth repeating," she said as she stood and grabbed her jacket off the coat tree. "I'm off to interview Reverend John Winters."

"The TV preacher?"

Amanda nodded. "He's speaking tonight at the MCI Center. I called and asked him for an interview this morning, so he's freed up sometime around ten. I'm really not sure about this guy, but it should be interesting. Want to come?"

"Sure," he said. "Give me a second to let April know. I'll meet you downstairs."

"Okay. Dana and Marv are coming too, along with Pete, so we'll bring the van around and pick you up curbside."

Moments later, they were on their way to the Renaissance Hotel, where Reverend John had rented a suite. As they entered the lushly appointed lobby with its crimson velvet sofas, Amanda noticed a tall, lanky man coming toward them. Although he was wearing an obviously expensive suit, it hung on his thin body like a sack.

"Ms. Fox?" he asked as he extended his hand. "I'm Benny McDuff, an associate with the Spirit of Truth Ministries."

Amanda clasped his hand. "Nice to meet you," she said.

"Reverend John is expecting you. May I show you to his suite?"

"Certainly."

There was an uncomfortable silence in the elevator as it climbed to the eighth floor.

After one knock, Benny inserted a keycard, opened the door, and stood back to allow Amanda, Mark, and the crew into the room. As he followed them in, Benny turned to lock and chain the door. Reverend John sat on a red velvet Queen Anne chair, and as they approached, he hefted himself up and came toward them.

"Ms. Fox," he said, taking her hand, "It is nice to meet you at last."

"Thank you," Amanda said as she tried to release her hand.

"I'd like you meet Mark Laux, the executive producer of 'Amanda Fox WeekEnd.'"

Reverend John finally let go of Amanda's hand to grasp Mark's. "It's an honor, sir." Mark only nodded and gave Reverend John a slight smile.

"And this is Pete Vargas, our cameraman, and Dana Wilson, who handles the lights, and finally Marv Thorn, our sound man. It will take us a few minutes to get set up." She quickly looked around the room. "The sofa and chair will work fine, if that works for you."

"Absolutely," he boomed. "Whatever you say. You're the boss." He walked over to the bar. "May I offer you something cold to drink while we're waiting? Let's see, we have Diet Coke, Diet Sprite, iced tea, and Perrier."

She glanced quickly at Mark, who didn't seem interested, and then at the others, who were busy setting up.

"No, I think we're fine, but thank you." She felt Benny McDuff's eyes on her and pivoted to face him. "So, Mr. McDuff, how long have you been working for the Spirit of Truth Ministries?"

"Oh, we go back a long way," Reverend John said as he poured himself a Perrier. "What is it, Benny? Twenty-nine years?"

"Thirty," Benny replied, without taking his eyes off of Amanda.

Amanda vowed not to show how uncomfortable Benny made her feel. "That's a long time," she said with a smile. "Where did you work before the Spirit of Truth Ministries?"

"Here and there," Benny said, unflinching.

Reverend John came over and patted Benny on the back. "Oh, Benny's just being modest. I'll tell you, though, it was my lucky day when he came to work for us. The Good Lord has given all of us our talents. Mine is ministering to the people, and Benny's a genius at handling our financial matters. I don't know what we would do without him," he said as he gave Benny a quick smile. "Well, are we about ready for this interview?" They settled into their positions, with Reverend John in the velvet chair. Dana started recording and cued Amanda.

"Reverend John," Amanda began, "I understand that you have actually seen and spoken to an angel. Can you tell me about it?"

As he described seeing the angel and her message to build a magnificent temple honoring God, tears welled in his eyes. "Ms. Fox, I want to tell you I feel so privileged and humbled that they chose me to deliver this message to the world."

"That's an amazing story, Reverend John. What did she look like?"

"She was so beautiful," he said as he looked into the camera. "She almost had a glow from within."

"And you said, after delivering her message, she flew away?"

"Oh, yes," he said in awe. "She spread her wings and silently flew back towards heaven."

"So, you're planning crusades across the United States to raise money for this temple?"

"Not only across America, but we have been called to take this message to the world. We have our first crusade at the MCI Center tonight at 7:30. Tickets are going fast, but I believe we still have a few left." He again looked at the camera. "I hope any of the good people listening will join us tonight. Just call the MCI Center box office. People are standing by right now, waiting for your call."

"So, there's a charge to come see you tonight?"

He gave her a sideways smile. "Just nominal, and that barely covers our expenses." He looked back at the camera. "What we're hoping for is that people will open their hearts to this magnificent undertaking and will want to be part of God's holy plan. We've done so much good in the world, including funding a children's wing at Mercy Hospital in Baton Rouge, but there's so much more to do. Our plan is to expand our help and presence throughout the world, just as God has ordained me to do."

Amanda forced a smile and said, "Reverend John, thank you for taking timeout of your busy schedule to speak with us."

"It has been my honor, Ms. Fox."

CHAPTER FOURTEEN

"Amanda," Mark said upon entering her office, "switch to CBS. They're reporting on the sightings."

She quickly punched the remote. Alan Frank, a senior reporter, was sitting across from another gentleman who was wearing a yarmulke.

"There are people recently in the news who have claimed not only that they have seen angels, but that God himself has chosen these people to deliver a message to mankind. Yet, there are many people who are insisting that this is nothing more than a hoax. Joining us now to talk about this in New York is ACLU attorney Victoria Davis-Smith, Pastor James Thomas from New Orleans, and Rabbi Alan Steinberg here in our studio."

"Pastor Thomas? That's our Pastor Thomas," Amanda said to Mark. "What's he doing on CBS?" Amanda sat down in a chair as she continued to watch.

"Pastor Thomas, let's begin with you. Wasn't it one of your parishioners who said she saw an angel?"

"Yes, Miss Ellie. She's a very special lady."

"And you believe her?"

"Yes, I believe her."

"But, reverend, if you hadn't been personally involved, do you think you'd feel the same way?"

"Yes," he said with certainty. "I have total faith in God, and I know all things are possible with Him."

"Come on," Victoria Davis-Smith shouted, "there's been no verification."

"Hold on a moment, Miss Davis-Smith. I promise you'll get the last word. But first let me ask you, Rabbi, do you think these angel sightings are real?"

"Well, Alan," the rabbi said with a smile, "I have to agree with Miss Davis-Smith. At the moment, there has been no verification. There's really a two-sided question here. If I tell you no, I don't think they're real, it sounds as if I don't believe in God, and of course I do. But we of the Jewish faith believe that many things have to happen before God returns and the Rapture occurs, and they simply haven't happened."

"What types of things?"

He laughed, "Well, I don't think there's time to cover our entire end-time beliefs, but of course one thing is the return of our land that was promised to us by God, and that has not happened."

"So, you think the whole thing is a hoax?"

"I don't know how they did it, but I think so, yes."

"Ms. Davis-Smith, let's go to you. We understand that the ACLU has come out very strongly against all the press coverage of angel sightings."

"Absolutely. The press is trying to create hysteria in America and throughout the world based solely on hearsay. There's been no proof. You know as well as I do that it's not a major deal to get two or three people, or ten or twelve for that matter, to come up with the same story. We believe that a certain religious group is behind this and we're planning a lawsuit to that effect."

"Could you elaborate on that?"

"No, I'm not at liberty to discuss the details. Let's just say that I have very reliable evidence that this is indeed a hoax."

"To what end?"

"It's politics, Alan, it always is. The Christian Coalition is pushing this to promote their agenda."

"Are you saying the Christian Coalition is behind this?"

"No, I didn't say that at all," she snapped. "I said there are others behind this, but it certainly plays into the hands of the Christian Coalition."

"Wow," Amanda said, "now there's a girl you'd like to take home to Mom." The ringing of the phone startled her.

"Amanda," April said. "I know you said to screen your calls about the angel sighting, but you might want to talk to this lady. She says her young daughter has seen an angel and would like to speak to you, but the scary thing is she says the angel gave her daughter predictions."

"Have her wait one minute and then ring her through." She looked at Mark. "Another one. This time it's a little girl who's seen an angel. I don't know, Mark. Maybe the ACLU attorney's right. Am I just creating hysteria with all these reports? I mean, good grief, now it's affecting kids."

Before Mark could respond, the call came through. Amanda took a deep breath and answered. "Amanda Fox."

"Ms. Fox?" the caller asked with a trace of a British accent.

"Yes, this is Amanda."

"My name is Caroline Ballard. My daughter, Katie, is nine. She told me that an angel came to see her and gave her a message. I've seen your reports on television and that's why I'm calling you."

"Mrs. Ballard, we've had literally hundreds of calls from people who claim they've seen angels and, unfortunately, many of the stories have turned out to be false. Please forgive me if I sound rude, but what makes your daughter's story different?"

The lady was quiet for a moment. "You'd have to know Katie. If ever there was an angel that walked on the earth, it's her. She's never told a tale in her life, so when she says an angel has visited her, I believe her. She said the angel has given her predictions of world events to come."

"What kind of world events?"

"I only know bits and pieces. It's important for you to hear the entire story, so it would be best if you talk to her about that."

"Would it be possible to bring her to Washington, D.C.? The network will pay your expenses."

"I'm afraid that wouldn't work. Katie's on dialysis and she needs her treatment."

Amanda closed her eyes for a moment as she let out a breath. "Let me see what I can do to work it out. May I have your phone number and address?" She made a quick note, then hung up and looked at Mark with faint amusement. "I know. Don't say it. Another wild goose chase."

Mark shrugged. "If you thought it was a wild goose chase, you wouldn't go."

She smiled. "Well then, what would you think about coming with me and chasing some wild geese in Canada?"

CHAPTER FIFTEEN

The afternoon sun glinted off Seattle's Lake Union as the floatplane lifted off for the 30 minute flight to Victoria, B.C. Amanda stretched, still trying to wake up from the long redeye flight from Washington. She looked over at Mark seated next to her, then at Pete across the aisle, and saw that they were both dozing. She flipped open her notepad and began jotting down her thoughts, trying to make some sense out of the last few weeks.

She began with Ellie LeBeaux, noting everything—from her mannerisms to her angel description to her religion. Then she did the same with Manuel Guzman and Reverend John Winters. Obviously, Reverend John's description differed from the others, but who's to say that doesn't make the story even more credible? If this were a planned hoax perpetrated by a group of people, wouldn't they all have the same story? Reverend John is certainly making money from this, but are the others part of a scheme to make him look more credible? None of these people are even the same religion.

Then there's Niko Gravari, who won't even return her calls. Amanda shrugged. Maybe he had decided at the last moment that he didn't want to be part of this, she thought. The last name she wrote was

Katie Ballard. If these people are using nine-year-old children for their own gain, they've crossed the line as far as Amanda was concerned.

She looked down at the myriad of islands that dotted Puget Sound below. From a distance she saw Vancouver Island and the glistening high-rises on the shore. The plane began its gradual descent and splashed down just inside of Victoria's harbor, waking both Mark and Pete. As they slowly idled to the dock, Mark glanced over at Amanda's open notebook.

"Figured it out yet?"

Amanda shook her head. "None of it makes any sense. Now that there's a child involved, it's even more of a mystery. I'd be willing to bet you almost anything that Reverend John is behind all of this, but why the little girl?"

"I don't know. People will do almost anything for money. Didn't you say the girl is on dialysis? That's got to be expensive. Canadian health care is poor at best, so maybe the family's desperate. Whatever, though, we'll know soon enough. How do you want to do this? Interview her first, then shoot it?"

"You know, I think it's better to just shoot it. It won't be live anyway and we can edit it later, but I think the best interview is usually the first one. If we do it twice, it will just sound rehearsed."

"Good enough," he said as he checked his watch. "It's 1:30. What time's the return flight?"

"We're booked on the four o'clock. That should give us plenty of time to find the house and talk to the girl. We can just grab a cab at the dock and maybe con the driver into waiting for us until we're finished."

"As long as you pay him well," Mark said with a smile.

Deplaning and going through customs took no more than fifteen minutes and they found a taxi immediately. After the equipment bags were loaded into the trunk, they climbed in and Amanda gave the driver the address.

"Oh sure," he said, "the Ballard's.

"You know them?" she asked, obviously surprised

"Oh, yeah," he said as he raised the flag on the meter. "Victoria's a small city. The locals pretty much know each other. I went to school with Caroline and Charley."

"So you know Katie?"

"Ah, yes. Lovely child. Poor thing, though, with her kidney problem."

"Yes, I heard about that," Amanda said. "It must be pretty expensive to be on dialysis."

"Especially here," the driver replied. "But we do what we can to help. A couple of times a year we have a fund-raiser." He laughed. "Well, it's more like a big party. We have it over at Topaz Park and the whole town comes. The ladies sell homemade cakes and pies and we have games and pony rides for the kids. All the proceeds go to Katie and her family to help pay for her dialysis."

"That's incredible," Amanda said.

"Nah," he said. "We all look out for each other."

Mark was staring forward with a look of contemplation. Feeling Amanda's eyes on him, he looked over and gave her a faint smile. They pulled up in the driveway and Mark asked the driver if he would wait for them if they paid for his extra time.

"Oh sure," he said, unloading the bags and camera equipment from the trunk. He helped them up to the house and rang the bell.

The door opened, revealing a young girl in a yellow dress with long blond hair. Standing behind her was a woman with curly red hair which was caught in a low ponytail by a blue bow that matched her pantsuit. When she saw the taxi driver, she broke into a warm smile.

"So you brought them, huh Tommy? Come in, please, all of you," she said as she opened the door wide.

Amanda matched her smile and extended her hand. "Mrs. Ballard, I'm Amanda Fox."

"It's so good to meet you. Please call me Caroline," she said, clasping Amanda's hand with both of hers. "I know it's not an easy trip, but I do thank you for coming."

Amanda stepped aside. "And this is our producer, Mark Laux."

Again, Caroline clasped her hands around Mark's hand. "So nice to meet you."

"Our cameraman, Pete Vargas," Amanda said. Caroline grasped Pete's hand in hers as she nodded. Amanda then looked down at the little girl peeking around her mother's skirt. "And you must be Katie."

"No," Caroline said. "This is Grace, our youngest daughter. She's a little shy," she added in a whisper. She gently pulled Grace in front of her. "Katie just came back from her treatment, and she's a bit tired right now, so she's resting on the sofa. Come, I'll introduce you."

They followed Caroline into the living room, where Katie was sitting on the sofa with a blanket tucked around her legs. The child was much smaller than her younger sister. Her pale skin was almost translucent and contrasted sharply with her red curly hair.

Her mother sat beside her on the sofa and put her arm around her. "Katie, this is Amanda Fox, the lady I told you about. She's come to hear your story about the angel."

Katie looked up at Amanda with her clear blue eyes. "Hello, Mrs. Fox."

Amanda smiled at the Mrs. title. "Hello," she said. "You can call me Amanda if you'd like. This is Mark and this is Pete. We've come to hear all about your angel and we'd like to tape this as we talk to each other. Would that be okay with you?"

Katie looked uncertain. Her mother turned to her and said, "Do you remember at the last picnic when Uncle Ned had his video camera? He recorded you and Grace and later you saw it on the television? It will be like that."

Katie looked over at Pete. "Is that your video camera?"

"Yeah," Pete said as he smiled at her. "It's just really big."

"Okay then," Katie said, looking back at Amanda.

"Can she stay where she is?" Caroline asked, "Or would you rather have her somewhere else?"

"She's just fine where she is," Amanda said. "I'll just sit on the other side of her."

As she sat next to Katie, Amanda turned to her and said. "Katie, in order for everyone to hear us really well, we're going to put a microphone on you and one on me." Mark clipped a tiny lapel mic on Katie's shirt and another on Amanda's jacket.

"They're really small, but really powerful. We don't want to miss anything you have to say. Now, what I'm going to do is simply ask you some questions and then I want you to just tell me what happened as you remember it. Are you ready?" Katie nodded. Amanda looked at Mark, who counted down from five with his fingers. At zero, the red light flashed on the camera. Mark held a board marked with the city and the date on it, and then the camera focused on Amanda.

"We're in Victoria, British Columbia, today with yet another angel sighting. Nine-year-old Katie Ballard has said that she has actually talked to an angel." She turned toward Katie and Pete pulled the camera back to include the two of them.

"Katie, tell us about your angel sighting. Where did this happen?"

Katie looked at Amanda, not the camera. "I was getting my treatment in the hospital."

"This treatment you're talking about is dialysis?" Katie nodded.

"How often do you go to the hospital?"

"Three times a week."

"When you're doing your dialysis treatment, how long are you in the hospital?"

"About two hours."

"So what happened on the day you saw the angel?"

"Mommy had gone down to the cafeteria, and I was in the room alone and I saw her."

"This was a lady angel?"

"No, it was a girl."

Amanda hesitated a moment before continuing. "Did this angel have wings?"

"Yes."

"What did she say to you?"

"She said God loves us, but she said that some people have not loved God, and she said that God is going to send a sign."

Surprised, Amanda hesitated for a moment. "What kind of sign?"

"She said God is going to send three earthquakes."

A chill ran through Amanda, but she tried to stay as professional as possible. "Did she say where these earthquakes would be?"

"The first one will be in Korea. Then a wall of water will hit China."

Amanda looked at her intently. "Did she tell you when?"

Katie nodded. "She told me it would be in seven days."

"What day did you see her?"

"Last Monday."

"So she said the earthquake in Korea will be next Monday?"

Katie nodded. "And she said those who believe will be saved."

Amanda was momentarily stunned by the enormity of this prediction that Katie repeated so simply. "And she said there would be others?"

"Yes. The second one will be in New York."

"New York? In New York City?" Amanda asked, clearly surprised.

"In New York," Katie repeated.

"Did she tell you when that one would be?"

"In three days after Korea."

"And where will the last one be?"

"In Iran, three days after New York."

"This must have been very scary for you."

Katie smiled. "No, because she told me not to be afraid. She said God loves me, but she told me God wants me to tell people to prepare themselves."

"Did she say anything else to you?"

Katie shook her red curls. "She just touched my face with the back of her finger and then she just disappeared." She looked up at Amanda with her clear blue eyes. "It's important to love God, isn't it?"

Amanda studied the little girl for a moment and then smiled softly. "Yes, Katie, it is."

CHAPTER SIXTEEN

On the ninth floor of the network corporate offices, Gabe Stein waited uncomfortably in the outer office of Martin Scolesco. The CEO of WNN had summoned him for a 10:00 a.m. meeting and Gabe knew, from prior experience, that it usually meant bad news. He checked his watch: 9:54. He looked up at Sally Ewolt, Mr. Scolesco's longtime secretary, trying to get a read on what was happening. Her face registered nothing but cool professionalism. Gabe had grabbed a magazine and begun thumbing through the pages, not really reading any of them, when the outer door opened and Fred Shelton, the senior vice president for public relations, walked in.

"Hi Sally, I have a ten o'clock appointment with Mr. Scolesco."

"Please have a seat, Mr. Shelton. I'll let him know you're here," Sally said.

He turned and saw that he was not alone. "Gabe," he acknowledged as he took a seat beside him.

"You too, huh? What's up?"

"No idea."

The phone rang. Sally spoke quietly and then replaced the receiver. "Mr. Scolesco will see you both now."

As they walked into the expansive office lined with photos and awards, Martin Scolesco sat behind his large mahogany desk. "Please have a seat," he said, gesturing to the two chairs in front of him. His suit jacket hung on a coat rack behind the desk, and his white shirt was characteristically rolled up at the sleeves. At sixty-seven, his early years as a newspaper editor had never left him, and he was still uncomfortable in the structure of a jacket.

"I had a phone call from Bartelli over at ConTel this morning. He said they're going to pull their ads," Scolesco said, looking at both of them over the rim of his glasses.

Fred was astounded, realizing that meant a loss of more than fifty million dollars a year to WNN. "Why?"

"That's what I want to know," Scolesco said, propping his elbows on the desk and clasping his hands in front of him. "What do you know about it, Gabe?"

Gabe Stein was basically the new kid on the block since he had only been with WNN for a year. He had been the vice president of advertising at CNC when a headhunter called and said WNN was looking for a new vice president of advertising and would he be interested? In a heartbeat, he left CNC and never looked back, until now. Suddenly, he knew his job was in jeopardy.

"I really don't know. I spoke with Bartelli last week and he didn't say a thing. I mean, this is a complete surprise."

"Fred?" Scolesco asked, turning away from Gabe.

"Well, theories only. Through the grapevine, I'm hearing that our over-reporting of the angel story is making some people nervous."

"What have you heard?"

"I don't know about ConTel, but I spoke to Don McCauley over at Minsinger yesterday. He said the angel sighting reports are beginning to irritate the execs. He said he wouldn't be surprised if Minsinger pulled their ads and went elsewhere."

"So," Scolesco said, tensing his jaw. "Now we're being told what we will or won't air." His eyes were cold as steel. "Looks like our back's against the wall on this one," he said as he waved his hand in a gesture of dismissal. "Go on back to work, but let me know immediately if you hear anything else."

After they left, he went to his bar and poured himself a glass of water. He walked over to the window, contemplating his next move. Martin was furious at the thought of being dictated to by sponsors, but revenues were revenues and he had a board of directors to answer to as well. The angel stories had to be axed immediately. He went back to the desk and punched the intercom. "Sally, get me Mark Laux."

"Sir, he's on assignment with Amanda Fox in Canada."

"Then leave a message on his cell. I want to see him the moment he returns."

CHAPTER SEVENTEEN

At 7:45 on Friday morning, Mary Beth Hodges sat at her computer, typing up the additions to the prayer list for Sunday's church service. This was the third time this week the Bethany Baptist Church bulletin had to be revised, due to fact that two church members had unexpectedly been admitted to the hospital. Additionally, there was a last-minute baptism scheduled for the new grandson of one of the elderly church members. Since Reverend Thomas' TV appearances, she knew the only way she could get any work done was to come in early when no one was around. The phones weren't ringing and it was blissfully quiet.

As she typed away, she heard the sound of a key turning the lock and looked up to see Priscilla Brown, one of the deacons of the church and head of the Flower Guild, coming through the opened door. "Mary Beth," Priscilla exclaimed in surprise, "what are you doing here so early?"

"Hi 'Cilla," she said with a resigned smile. "Well, between fending off phone calls from the press on Miss Ellie's angel sighting, and just normal church work, I feel like all I'm doing this week is just catching up. I thought I'd come in when it was quiet to get some things finished up."

"You're still getting calls from those news people?"

Mary Beth let out an exasperated sigh and nodded. "And poor Miss Ellie, they call her day and night—and it's not just press people. She even had phone calls from people threatening her. She's at the point where she can't even answer her phone anymore, so they call here."

Priscilla looked worried. "Have they threatened you?"

"No," Mary Beth said, "not really. I'm just surprised how some people can be so angry about this."

"Maybe their anger is just from fear, but that doesn't make any difference. Those people can still be dangerous, so you just keep that door locked when you're here by yourself."

She smiled. "I will. So, is there anything I can do to help you this morning?"

"No, you've got enough to do. I've just unloaded a van full of flowers for Margie Andrew's wedding tomorrow. I thought I'd get started on the boutonnieres and get those finished so when Constance and Patty come, we can all work on the arrangements. But I need the key for the storage closet."

"Sure," Mary Beth said, opening her drawer. "I've got it right here."

"Thanks, and don't forget to lock the door after me," Priscilla said as she was leaving the office. "I'm going to do the same in the Parish Hall, so call me if you need me."

Mary Beth pushed herself away from the desk, went to the door and locked it once again. It was terrible for a church to operate with locked doors, she thought, as she went back to her desk and resumed working. After an hour, the bulletins were finished, as well as the insert for the baptism ceremony. She was just printing them when she heard sounds outside the door. Priscilla must need something else, she thought, as she went toward the door to unlock it.

In the Parish Hall, Priscilla wrapped the last white rose boutonniere with florist tape, added a pearl pin and laid it in the box containing the other boutonnieres and corsages. As she picked up a pew vase to begin the first arrangement, she heard a thunderous boom.

Good heavens, what on earth? Fear gripped her as she ran to the phone to call Mary Beth. The line was dead. Without wasting a second, she unlocked the door and ran to the church office where she saw the carnage. The door was gone and the office was in shambles.

"Mary Beth," she yelled as she ran inside, and pushed her way in past the debris, where she found her lying under what was left of her desk. "Oh, Mary Beth" she gasped as she tossed aside the fragments of metal, the splinters of wood, and the blood soaked papers that covered her. Mary Beth was absolutely still. "No," screamed Priscilla, "God, please no."

Tears were rolling down Priscilla's face when she thought she heard a soft moan. "Mary Beth?" Pricilla's heart was pounding. "Hold on. I'll help you. I'll get help."

"What on earth happened?" Constance Reuther yelled as she stood outside the church office. "Priscilla?"

"Call 911," Priscilla screamed. "Mary Beth needs an ambulance now. Then call Reverend Thomas." She took off her sweater, put it over Mary Beth, and then cradled Mary Beth's head under her arm. "It's okay, honey," she said softly. "Help is coming, and I won't leave you. Hold on. Just hold on."

CHAPTER EIGHTEEN

"Ladies and gentlemen, this is your captain speaking. We have been informed that Washington, D.C. is currently experiencing some rain showers. For the next hour or so until landing, there might be some bumpy air, so I would like you all to return to your seats and securely fasten your seat belts."

Amanda pulled her seat belt tighter just as a violent bump shook the plane, spilling her drink partly on her and mostly on Mark's shirt.

"Sorry," she said, offering Mark her napkin. "At least now you know why I never order anything on a plane but club soda. It never stains and dries quickly."

He shivered. "It's just blasted cold in the meantime," he said, laughing.

Amanda glanced out the window at the tall gray and white clouds around them. They looked ominous, and her mind immediately went back to Katie's prediction of the earthquakes.

"Mark," she said as she tucked a strand of hair behind her ear and leaned toward him, "I've been thinking about Katie's interview, and I'll be honest. I'm not even sure where to go with it. If we show it as is, you know this will cause a panic."

"I know," Mark said quietly.

"I keep wondering if Reverend John is behind this, or maybe someone at another network is trying to destroy us. I mean, if we show the tape on Katie and nothing happens except panic in New York, then WNN is going to take the hit and we're going to have some major problems."

"Are you saying you don't want to show it?"

"I don't know," she said, waving her hand. "What if she's wrong?"

His eyes came up and studied her face. "What if she's right?"

"Then we'll be heroes," she said with a slight smile.

"Or fools pounding the pavement looking for other jobs. Besides, there may not be such a panic after all. The odds of an earthquake hitting New York are slim at best, so really, how many people are going to buy it?"

Amanda looked out the rain-streaked window. She sat back in her seat and remembered what Katie had said: "Those who believe will be saved."

Despite the storm, the plane touched down ten minutes early. As it taxied, they both turned on their cell phones and retrieved their messages. Amanda grabbed her book to jot down phone numbers, then stopped as she listened, biting down hard on her lower lip.

"I can't believe this," she said.

"What's the matter?"

"It was April. The church has been bombed. Bethany Baptist in New Orleans—Miss Ellie's church."

"When?"

"This morning. She said the secretary is in intensive care. She didn't say anything about Pastor Thomas or Miss Ellie. I've got to call him. Are you heading home?"

"No. Scolesco wants to see me, and I quote, "The minute I arrive back in Washington."

Amanda frowned. "What's that all about?"

He shrugged slightly. "I'll soon find out. Want to share a cab?"

When they arrived at the studios, Mark left immediately for his meeting and Amanda headed for her office. She hung her coat on the rack and grabbed her cell phone. Checking her call log, she touched the number of Bethany Baptist. After three rings the call was picked up.

"Bethany Baptist," Pastor Thomas said.

"Pastor Thomas," Amanda said, surprised. "It's Amanda. I really wasn't expecting you to be there. In fact, I wasn't even sure the phone would ring. I just returned from Canada and I had a message about the bombing and Mary Beth. How is she?"

"I've just come from the hospital and she's doing surprisingly well. Still in critical care, but they feel that she can be put into a regular room by tomorrow if she continues to improve."

"What happened?"

"Apparently, someone put a bomb in the trash can just outside the office door. Mary Beth had come in early to get some work done and was standing by her desk when the bomb exploded. The force blasted the door right at her. Fortunately, two of our church members who were here working on wedding flowers heard the explosion and found her. They immediately called 911 and then me. By the time I arrived, they were just loading her into the ambulance."

"Have you any idea who may have done it?"

"No," he said quietly. "The police and the FBI are working on it. But I can tell you one thing, Ms. Fox. We refuse to be intimidated by anyone. Whoever did this will be caught and punished."

"This is my hope as well," Amanda said. "I realize it's a difficult time for you right now, but it might help for you to do a live interview from the church tonight with a plea to anyone who may have seen anything suspicious to contact the police."

Pastor Thomas was quiet for a moment and then said, "For Mary Beth's sake, I'll be glad to do it."

"Good. The public can often be a big help. I'll call our affiliate and make the arrangements and they'll give you a call. I just wish there was something else I could do for you."

"I appreciate it, but there may be something I can do for you. I happened to see your interview with Reverend John."

"Yes, about his angel sighting."

"Yes, well, my association with John Winters goes back many

years, and I believe there's some information you should know about him. He's not exactly what he appears to be."

"What do you mean?"

"He was involved many years ago in a scheme to defraud the public. The FCC finally pulled his broadcast license."

"How do you know this?"

"I was one of several to testify against him in court." Amanda was silent for a moment. "Just know who you're dealing with," Pastor Thomas continued. "I absolutely do believe in the angel sightings and I applaud your efforts in reporting honestly about them, but I feel that Reverend John just may be taking advantage."

After she hung up, Amanda's mind was racing. Now she knew there was more to the story of Reverend John. How it all tied into these angel sightings was the story that needed to be told. She punched her intercom. "April, could you step in here a minute?" She pulled out a legal pad and started making notes.

A moment later, she heard a knock. "Hi," Amanda said, gesturing for April to have a seat. "I need you to do a couple of things for me. We need to get a live feed from New Orleans with Pastor Thomas for the show tonight. Call WVUE and set it up for 8:00 pm New Orleans time, at Bethany Baptist Church."

She hurriedly wrote out a phone number on the yellow pad, ripped it off, and handed it to April. "They need to contact him at this number. The second thing is that we need to get a little more information on Reverend John."

"Reverend John? Why?"

"Well, it seems that there's more to this guy than most people know. I want you to do some digging. Check his background. Check the legal records in Louisville and see if his name pops up, and while you're at it, check on Benny McDuff. He's an associate of Reverend John's."

"What am I looking for?" April asked, jotting down the names.

"Well, if my information is right, you're looking for fraud and corruption, and it seems to be tied in to these angel sightings."

April looked at her in surprise. "Geez, I've watched him for years on TV. I've even sent money."

"My point exactly," Amanda said. "If something illegal is going on here, we need to let the public know about it. See what you can find."

"Okay," she said as she stood. "By the way, Pete just called from the editing room. There's something on that tape from Canada that he wants you and Mark to see."

"Did he say what it was?"

"He just said he'll wait for you there."

"Okay, I'll go right now. When Mark gets back from his meeting, just tell him where I am."

As Amanda waited for the elevator, her mind was filled with Mary Beth, the bombing, and of Pastor Thomas' past association with Reverend John. She knew she needed to go back to New Orleans and do a follow-up story. The elevator bell sounded, jarring her thoughts. As the door opened, Mark was just stepping out with a grim look on his face. "Just coming to see you," he said.

"Let's talk in the elevator. Pete wants us to look at something on the tape of the little girl." She stopped, as she searched his face. "What on earth happened? Are you fired? Am I?"

"Not yet," he said with a bland half smile as he punched the elevator button. "But it looks like the angel stories are nixed."

"What?" Amanda exclaimed loudly.

"It seems that sponsors are canceling on us. We've already lost over a hundred million."

"Why would they pull out?" Amanda walked to the other side of the elevator and crossed her arms. "I can't believe Martin Scolesco would cower to anybody dictating what we can and can't report on.

"Looks like he did."

"But this is so important, especially with the bombing. How can we possibly stop now? This is so much bigger than we think it is. I just spoke to Pastor Thomas and apparently he was partly responsible for the FCC pulling Reverend John's license some years ago."

"Do you think he's up to his old tricks again?"

"Absolutely—and I have a feeling this is just the tip of the iceberg.

April is doing research, not only on the good Reverend but on Benny McDuff too."

The elevator door opened, revealing a long hallway. As they made their way to the editing room, Amanda looked over at Mark. "Think it would help if we both went back to Scolesco and told him what I've found out?"

"Doubt it," he said as they walked into the editing room

"What's up, Pete?"

"You gotta see this. Okay, Joe, run it again."

The interview was exactly the same as they remembered.

"So?" asked Amanda.

"Wait," Pete said. "It's coming."

Amanda was sitting next to Katie asking her questions, but when they reached the part where Katie was telling about the predictions, a blur appeared between them.

"What's that?" Mark asked.

"Keep watching," Pete said.

As all four watched, the blur began to take the form of a little girl sitting between Amanda and Katie. She was in a white gown and her wings were folded behind her. Her hair was blond and curly. As Katie was speaking, the little girl was looking at her and holding her hand.

"My God," Amanda said softly.

"I know," Pete whispered coarsely.

"Has this tape been with you all the time?" Mark asked Pete.

"Never out of my sight. I brought it here as soon as we landed."

Amanda looked at Mark. "Think we can get Scolesco to change his mind now?"

Mark grabbed the phone and dialed Martin's extension. "I'm sorry Mr. Scolesco has already left," Sally said.

"I need to reach him," Mark said urgently. "Can you have him call me on my cell?"

"Well, he's already taken the helicopter to Dulles and then he'll be enroute to Paris for several hours. He's left orders that he's not to be disturbed. Is there something I can help you with?"

"No," Mark said with a slight touch of exasperation. "Thanks, Sally." He clicked off the phone and sat deep in thought.

"Mark?" Amanda asked after a moment. "What are you thinking?"

He looked up at her and smiled. "I'm just wondering where we'll end up working after I get us both fired."

"You want to show the tape on tonight's show?"

"Yeah, I do," he said softly, "I don't think there's a choice."

Amanda returned his smile. "I don't either."

CHAPTER NINETEEN

Forty-three thousand feet above the dark Atlantic Ocean, Martin Scolesco was just being served his after-dinner drink. Normally, he paid little attention to the trappings of wealth, but this new Gulfstream 650 absolutely took his breath away. As he sipped cognac and nestled back in his plush leather chair, he glanced around the cabin's spacious interior. Rich burl wood tables accented by touches of twenty-four karat gold set off the luscious butter-cream-yellow chairs and sofas. Definitely eye candy, it was a vision to behold.

Beyond the décor, though, he respected the technology. Unlike WNN's previous Gulfstream, this plane was fully equipped for intercontinental operations. Its state-of-the-art audio, video, and communications system included TV, WiFi, Airshow, and satellite phones.

No matter where he was in the world, he was never out of touch with either the network's operations or any of WNN's affiliates. Three flat-screen televisions, mounted high in the cabin directly across from him, were on and muted. The first was set to WNN, the second to CNC and the third to NBC.

As he sipped his cognac, he watched the closed-captioned crawl on each of the channels, and smiled when WNN went to commercial and ran a ConTel ad. It had taken a lot of promises and, unfortunately, some rate cutting, but Martin had finally been able to get ConTel back.

As an old news editor, though, it still galled him to be dictated to, but business was business and profits can't be made without advertising dollars. He saw that Amanda's show was just coming on, so he pressed the buttons on the side of his chair to un-mute WNN.

"As we go to air tonight, New Orleans is still reeling from a church bombing. Pattie Johnson of WVUE is at the scene right now. Pattie, what can you tell us?"

"Amanda, I'm here with Pastor James Thomas, the minister of Bethany Baptist Church. Pastor, the scene here is pretty devastating. I understand your secretary was working here in the office."

For the next several minutes, Pastor Thomas recounted the scene he found this morning and then reported on Mary Beth's condition.

Scolesco watched with interest, fully aware of Pastor Thomas's connection with the New Orleans angel sighting. Much to his relief, however, the concentration was on the church bombing and nothing was said about angels.

"Thanks for the report, Pattie," Amanda said. "We're putting the New Orleans police department's phone number on the screen right now. If anyone has any knowledge about this bombing or has seen anything unusual in the vicinity of Bethany Baptist Church, we ask you to please call. We have to go to a quick break, and we'll be back shortly."

So far so good, thought Martin as he muted the television and rang for the flight attendant.

"Another cognac, Mr. Scolesco?"

"No, Anne," he said, handing her the empty glass. "Just a cup of coffee. Black."

Within seconds she returned with a gold rimmed cup and saucer and a small pot of coffee. "If you need anything else, please let me know."

Amanda again appeared on the screen. He poured himself a cup and took a small sip as he un-muted the television.

"...in Victoria, British Columbia. We spoke to Katie yesterday morning." Amanda waited as they rolled the tape. As Martin watched, his initial astonishment turned into a slow rage at being so blatantly ignored. By the end of the interview, he was beyond furious. He grabbed the satellite phone and punched in WNN's number.

"Get me the control booth. Now!" As he waited, he watched the end of the tape and noticed a white blur on the screen. Fury turned into rage as he realized they had not only defied him, but they hadn't even bother to edit the tape!

Amanda again appeared on the screen. She seemed visibly shaken and hesitated a moment. "Uh, my apologies, ladies and gentlemen, there seemed to be a problem with the quality of the tape." Trying to regain herself she cleared her throat and continued. "If what Katie has predicted is true then the first earthquake will happen in Korea three days from the time of this interview, which would be Monday. I certainly hope she's wrong for all our sakes. We'll be right back."

"What are you doing, Laux?" Martin screamed. "Just what part of 'forget the angel reports' did you not understand? Have you any idea what position you've put us in now? Not just with our sponsors, but, my God man, this little stunt is going to cause a worldwide panic. What are you thinking?"

Amanda called the control booth. "What happened to the tape?"

Pete signaled to Tim Breton, the technician, that he'd pick up the call. "Amanda, it's Pete. No idea what happened. The whole thing just went to fuzz."

"Where's Mark?"

"On the phone with Scolesco."

"From the plane?"

"Tim just gave me the signal. You're back on in ten."

Mark shook his head as he listened to Scolesco's ranting.

"So, what have you got to say for yourself?"

"I tried to reach you, but you were out of contact, and seeing what I saw, I made a judgment call. I felt it was best to air the tape," Mark said quietly.

"What did you see?" Scolesco demanded.

Mark rubbed his forehead and let out a breath. "I saw—we saw an angel sitting next to the little girl."

"An angel? What do you mean you saw an angel? If you're trying to give me a coronary, well by heaven, you're doing a great job."

"There were actually four of us who saw it on the tape after we got back to the studio, and now," Mark said as his voice began to fall off, "it's not there."

"I don't know who's trying to pull what, but I'm sure going to find out. As of now, you and Amanda Fox are on immediate suspension and I swear, if I hear one more thing about angel sightings, not only will you be fired, but you will be sued."

The line went dead, and Mark clicked off his phone. He sat back in his chair and watched the rest of Amanda's show, knowing full well that this could be her last one at WNN. It was his decision that put her in this position, and his guilt was gnawing at him.

The floor director signaled Amanda that she had only one minute left. This was the time that she always read e-mails from the listeners.

"From Connie M. in Davenport, Iowa: 'Amanda, thank you for bringing religion back to America with your reports on angel sightings. We're praying for you.'

Thank you, Connie," Amanda said. "I'm just trying to get to the bottom of this story.

"Ms. Fox, Enough already of trying to stir people up with all this angel stuff. Admit it now; aren't you just trying to get ratings with all this sensationalizing?'-Ned Moft, Albany, New York.

"No, Mr. Moft, we at WNN News strive to bring you the truth. We would never discredit ourselves or demean our audience with sensational stories."

Amanda read aloud the next e-mail: "Ms. Fox, Do you really expect us to believe that the world is coming to an end just because a few people, who may well have tried to get publicity for themselves, have said so?' – Dan Martinez, Vacaville, California.

"No, Mr. Martinez, I'm not here to tell you what to believe. I'm only here to report the facts as a reporter," Amanda said evenly, looking into the camera.

"And from Meridian, Idaho: 'Ms. Fox, with the state that our world is in today, I don't blame God for being unhappy with us.'- Georgiana Bascomb.

"Indeed, Ms. Bascomb, indeed," Amanda said. "If you care to send us an e-mail, the address is at the bottom of your screen. Please include your name and town. This is Amanda Fox. Have a good evening."

As soon as the camera light went out, Amanda rushed to the control booth.

"What happened to the tape?" She saw the somber look on Mark's face and stopped. "What? Scolesco? What happened, Mark?"

He looked at her with a wry smile. "It looks like we're on vacation."

Amanda frowned, "We're fired?"

"No," Mark said, his tone apologetic. "Suspended."

"For how long?"

"Well, he left that part kind of open ended."

"What about the story?"

"Ah, well, he did say something about that," he said with quiet emphasis. "He told me that if either of us said anything further about the angels that not only will we be fired, but we'll also be sued."

"Sued?" Amanda said, her surprise turning to anger. "Sued? What could he sue us for?"

"I'm not even sure he knows, but believe me, he and his army of lawyers will figure out something."

"This is incredible; especially now when we're so close. I think we're on a good trail with Reverend John. You know he's faking it for the money, and I think with Pastor Thomas' help, I'll be able to prove it. And what about Katie's predictions? What if they're real? Maybe I'm losing it, but I know we all saw something on that tape."

"Amanda," Mark cautioned. "Let it go."

"No," she said with fierce determination. "I can't"

"Listen, this isn't worth your job. I've already caused you enough problems by getting you suspended. I'm not going to let you get fired."

Amanda went over and sat in one of the technician's chairs. She took a deep breath trying to calm down. "Maybe you're right," she said at last. "Maybe I do need a vacation."

"Good," he said with a slight smile. "Where are you going?"

She leveled her eyes at him. "Louisiana."

CHAPTER TWENTY

The old church door creaked softly as Amanda slipped into Bethany Baptist. Fortunately, the choir was leading the parishioners in a resounding rendition of "Great and Mighty Is Our God." Amanda was able to sit in a pew at the back of the church with only a few people noticing her arrival. An older black lady wearing a dark blue dress with a matching hat smiled and handed Amanda her hymnal, which was opened to the song. Then she quickly picked up another hymnal for herself and joyously began singing again.

It was easy to be caught up in the room's energy as over a thousand worshippers sang and swayed to the music. The large church was stark, with its off-white walls and dark walnut pews. Sun had broken through the morning clouds and was softly filtering through the multi-paned windows, throwing streams of light on the parishioners and the choir's deep red robes. Reverend Thomas was standing off to the right in front of his high-backed walnut chair, singing along with the choir without the benefit of the hymnal.

After the final 'amen' was sung, Pastor Thomas walked up to the pulpit and opened his Bible. "Let us pray." All heads bowed. "Heavenly Father, we thank you for bringing us through this tribulation and for sparing Mary Beth Hodges. We ask that you continue to be with her and give her strength and health day by day. Only you in your wisdom know what compelled this evil act, but we ask that you forgive the ones responsible and bring them back into the light. We love you and praise you. Amen."

Several more 'amens' were heard throughout the congregation, then the church was quiet as Pastor Thomas took a moment in silent prayer. Seconds later he looked up at the watchful faces in front of him. Despite the shadows of fatigue under his eyes, his voice was strong and sure as he said, "Good morning." The congregation returned his greeting.

"At 7:30 this morning, I went to the hospital and saw Mary Beth. I told her how all of you have participated in prayer circles for her and she asked me to thank you. She's weak, but she's getting stronger by the moment, and I know it's because of you and our most merciful God."

"Earlier this week, I had planned to bring you the message of the prodigal son. Since this horrible bombing, I wasn't certain if this was what you needed to hear right now. But the more I thought about it, the more I realized the importance of this parable, especially now," he said as he rested on his elbows and clasped his hands in front of him.

"We read in St. Luke, chapter fifteen, verses eleven through thirty-two, the parable of the prodigal son. The story begins with a wealthy man who had two sons. In that day and age, even as now, an inheritance does not go to the sons until after the death of the father. But the younger son, who was very spoiled, demanded to have his inheritance early. Not asked, but demanded. 'Give me, give me, give me. I have a right to it,' the son said. He was tired of his father's rules and he wanted to go out in the world and experience life for himself. The father, who was a kind man, but also a very wise man, did as the son demanded. And so, the son left."

"The son traveled far and wide and experienced all of life's sensual pleasures. Without rules and regulations to follow, he did as he wished and spent heavily along the way. One day, he opened his purse and found that it was empty. Where his prudent father had very deep pockets, his were empty, with no hope now of even an inheritance. He became so hungry he began eating the food that was left in the pig's trough. The Bible says that at last, when he was so despondent, that he came to himself and had a desire to return to his father, if only to be a servant of his. He knew his father treated his servants better than anyone was treating him. So, he went home."

"His wise father patiently waited for his return and when he saw his son come over the hill, he ran to him with his arms wide open and embraced him. The younger son told him he was not worthy since he had sinned against him and against heaven, but the father welcomed him home and said, 'You were dead, but are now alive. You were lost, but now you are found. It is truly a time of celebration.'"

Pastor Thomas' tone turned somber. "We are a world of prodigal sons and prodigal daughters. We have strayed from our Father's rules and regulations, from his commandments. We have not honored God, we have not honored our own mothers and fathers, we have stolen, we have taken lives, we have been envious, we have committed adultery, and we have lied. In spite of all this, our Father in heaven loves us. He is patiently waiting for us to come back to Him so that he can open His arms and once again embrace us." He closed his Bible and smiled at the congregation. "Let us pray."

Amanda bowed her head and listened to Pastor Thomas' prayer, a suddenly a tear rolled down her cheek. Something stirred deep within as she thought of her father, her brother, and of her own distant relationship with God. After the prayer the organist began playing the final hymn. Amanda wiped the tear from her cheek and opened the hymnal to "Amazing Grace," this time singing with a new depth of understanding.

As the congregation filed out, each member stopping to greet Pastor Thomas, Amanda waited her turn in line. When she finally reached him, she reached out to shake his hand. "Ms. Fox," he said with surprise, "I'm so glad you could join us today."

"Thank you for such a wonderful sermon," Amanda said. "There are some things I'd like to talk to you about. Would you be available tomorrow?"

"Of course," he said. "I'll be here by eight trying to sift through what is left of my office. Come over when you can."

As she turned to leave, she spotted Ellie LeBeaux in a small crowd just outside of the church. Amanda felt uneasy, wondering if Ellie blamed her for the church bombing. Her choices were to quickly and quietly go back to her car in the parking lot or go over and say hello, but the choice was made for her when Ellie looked up and waved.

"Ms. Fox, how nice to see you again," Ellie said, extending her hand.

"How are you Ellie?" Amanda asked warmly.

"Very well, thank you. I'd like you to meet my daughter, Georgia Fontaine."

"Very nice to meet you," Amanda said, taking her hand. She looked back at Ellie. "This is unfortunately a sad time for your church."

"Yes, it is."

"Ellie, I'm so sorry if my interview with you was the cause of this."

Ellie shook her head slightly and gave Amanda a smile. "It's not your fault. Evil exists, Ms. Fox. The enemy is never happy unless they make others unhappy. Fortunately, our Mary Beth was saved and for that, we are all grateful."

"Yes, absolutely."

"I've been watching your reports of the other angel sightings, Ms. Fox. I believe our world has reached a most crucial turning point, the ultimate decision between good and evil."

Amanda looked into her eyes. "I heard that it will be a battle. You think it's simply a decision?"

"I didn't say it was simple, but yes, I think it will be a decision. God has always given us that power and that will be our ultimate salvation or undoing."

Amanda glanced at Georgia and saw that she had the same steadfast strength as her mother. "You must be very proud of your mother," she said

"Yes, I am."

Amanda turned back to Ellie. "I'm so glad to have seen you again. I'll say a prayer for Mary Beth."

PAMELA YOUNG

Ellie smiled. "And you will be in our prayers, Ms. Fox."

When Amanda returned to her hotel room, thoughts of Ellie, her daughter, and Pastor Thomas' sermon raced through her mind. Ellie had said our world is at a crucial turning point. Why now? From the beginning of time, we've had hateful, destructive wars—not only in the name of politics, but of religion as well. And with each war, our weapons have become more and more powerful.

Yes, Amanda thought, I suppose it's true that we've taken God's beautiful world and polluted it. And it's also true that our Western world has become more and more shameful and permissive and that the Eastern world has become terror ridden to the point where religions teach their children to kill people who do not believe as they do. Maybe Ellie's right. Maybe God's just fed up. Amanda felt a chill and wrapped herself in a sweater.

She thought of Pastor Thomas, his prodigal son sermon, and how we've all distanced ourselves from God's laws—pretending that the old teachings weren't important. She took a deep breath and thought of her own father. Suddenly, she felt an overwhelming urge to call him. As she dialed the number, she had no idea what she was going to say, but it didn't really matter.

"Hi, Dad."

"Amanda?" he asked, surprised. "You sound different. You okay?"

"Yeah, I'm fine," she said softly. "You may find this hard to believe, but I just came from church."

Her father listened in silence.

"Yeah," she continued. "And it was really good. I'm in New Orleans right now. Remember the first angel sighting I reported on? Ellie LeBeaux? It was her church. I was actually down here investigating a story. I hadn't really planned on attending church, but I wanted see what Bethany Baptist was all about. I've spoken to Pastor Thomas several times before, but I've never seen him give a sermon and," she stopped for a moment, "he was amazing."

"How so?"

"I don't know. There was such energy in the church and when he spoke about the prodigal son, it really blew me away."

"What did he say?"

"Well, he told the parable and then he compared it to the world today. He talked about prodigal sons and prodigal daughters and how we've strayed from the laws of God, and I thought about you and how you used to tell us that the Ten Commandments weren't ten suggestions. Remember?" She laughed softly.

"Yes, I remember."

"Well, I just wanted to call you and tell you that you were right."

Again, there was silence from her father.

"And," she said as her voice broke. "I just wanted to tell you that I love you."

"I love you, too, Amanda," he whispered.

"I've got some things to do here, but I'll try to get home soon."

"Looking forward to it. Your brother misses you, and so do I."

"I miss you guys, too."

CHAPTER TWENTY-ONE

W hen Amanda arrived at 9:10 a.m., Pastor Thomas and five other church members were going through papers and inspecting books that could be salvaged and re-shelved. "My goodness," she said surveying the damage.

"Good morning, Ms. Fox," he said as he put another book back in the bookcase. His black pants and shirt were covered in a gray dust. "You've come just in time to rescue me."

"Are you sure you don't want me to pitch in?"

"Well," he laughed, "You're hardly dressed for it," he said looking at her tan slacks and tan silk shirt, "but I thank you for the offer. Besides, look at this good crew here. We'll have this finished in no time. I thought it might be easier to talk in the library, if you'll just step this way." He walked over papers and books and guided her down a hallway to a small room. The walls were lined with bookcases from floor to ceiling. The only other furniture was a wooden table surrounded by eight wooden chairs.

"Please, have a seat," he said as he pulled a chair out for her and sat down across from her. "Now what can I do for you?"

"Actually, there are several things I need to talk to you about. First, though, I have to tell you how much your sermon meant to me." She hesitated before continuing. "It's good to reestablish family connections."

He looked at her questioningly.

She shook her head slightly. "It's fine. I just wanted to say thank you for that."

"You're very welcome," he said warmly.

"And," she continued, "there's been another angel sighting, but this one is different. A little girl in Victoria, British Columbia claimed that an angel told her to expect three earthquakes."

Pastor Thomas' eyes widened. "When?"

"She said the first was going to happen in Korea in three days. That was last Friday, so if she's right, it will happen today."

"And the others?"

"She said the second one will be in New York, three days later.

"New York City?"

"She just said New York."

"And the last?"

"In Iran in three more days."

Pastor Thomas sat back in his chair, trying to absorb what he just heard. He looked at Amanda. "Did you find this little girl believable?"

"I really did, but still it's a lot to believe, and I wasn't thoroughly convinced until we came back to the studio and ran the tape." Amanda hesitated as she looked down and then back at Pastor Thomas. "When I did the interview I was sitting on the sofa with the little girl sitting beside me, but when we ran the tape, there was an angel sitting between us looking at the little girl and holding her hand."

Pastor Thomas was too stunned to speak.

"I reported the angel sighting on my show Friday night and ran the interview, but when we televised it, the angel wasn't there, even though all of us in the editing room had seen her only moments before." She clasped her hands in front of her as she looked at Pastor Thomas. "This is all so unbelievable, I know, and yet I saw her."

Pastor Thomas took a deep breath. "And so a little child shall lead them," he said softly, almost to himself.

The jarring ringtone of Amanda's phone interrupted them. "I'm so sorry, let me turn this off," she said as she grabbed her phone

"No, take it. It's fine."

"Amanda Fox," she said. "Hi April." Amanda grabbed a pad from her purse and quickly made notes. "Which bank is that?" She asked as she continued to write. "Okay, got it. Anything yet on Benny McDuff?" She paused as she listened. "Really? Which prison? Thanks, April. Terrific work." She closed her phone and looked up at Pastor Thomas. "Well, I was going to tell you that we're doing some checking on Reverend John. It seems that your feeling about him was right. I don't know how we can prove it yet, but I think this man, and perhaps his associate, is really running a con operation and the public needs to be aware of it."

"Fortunately, Ms. Fox, you're in a position to do just that."

She shook her head regretfully. "I wish I could, but I'm actually on suspension at the moment."

"Suspension?" he asked, clearly surprised. "Why?"

"It seems that some sponsors are leaning heavily on the network to stop my reports on angel sightings. I'm actually under orders to stop all investigations." She shrugged and smiled slightly. "If WNN knew that I was here talking to you, I'd probably be fired."

Pastor Thomas sat back in his chair and returned her smile. "And yet here you are."

Her expression grew more serious. "I have to. I need to find out the answers for myself. I did see the angel on the tape with the little girl. I really saw her; and with the exception of Reverend John, I absolutely believe the others I've interviewed have told me the truth. God is real. He's here, and He's talking to us. How can I possibly not continue with this story?"

Pastor Thomas looked down at the table for a long moment and then back at Amanda. "Belief is a wonderful thing, Ms. Fox. What can I do to help you?"

"I need to know more about Reverend John."

.   .   .

Just past one o'clock, Amanda parked her car in front of the Spirit of Truth Church in Baton Rouge. She sat for a moment as she scanned the massive white brick building with its two-story columns. Wide steps led to a verandah that spanned the length of the building and, arched above the double French door, the Spirit of Truth Church sign was spelled out in ten-inch-high gold letters. To the left of the door was a pedestal holding a bronzed bust of Reverend John. This is too good, she thought. She had to see more.

As she walked up the stairs, she saw a plaque at the base of the statue which read, "To our beloved Reverend John from his faithful congregation. July 6, 1993." She tried the door, but it was locked. Not surprising, she thought, it was Monday afternoon. But, still, she was here and it might be interesting to look around. She walked down the steps and crossed a wide stretch of lawn leading toward the rear of the building. There she found a children's play area with swing sets, a basketball court, a tennis court, and a fenced area enclosing an Olympic-sized swimming pool.

"May I help you with something?"

Startled, Amanda turned to see Benny McDuff. Quickly regaining her composure, she held out her hand. "Mr. McDuff, how nice to see you again. Amanda Fox with WNN," she reminded him. "We met when I interviewed Reverend John in Washington."

He narrowed his eyes and shook her hand. "Yes, Miss Fox, I remember you. I'm surprised to see you here."

"Well, I was in New Orleans and I thought I would come up and say hello to Reverend John."

"He's not here," he snapped.

She smiled. "You have a beautiful church, and the grounds are lovely."

"Thank you," he said without returning her smile.

"Is it as beautiful inside?"

"It's very nice," he replied curtly. "I'm sorry I can't show you around. I'm on my way to a meeting. Perhaps, if you had called ahead, we might have been able to arrange something."

"Well, yes, I understand," she said as she extended her hand. "It was good to see you again and please tell Reverend John I stopped by."

He firmly clasped her hand and gave her a half smile. "You can count on it. Have a nice day."

She returned to her car and noticed Benny still watching as she drove away. Shuddering at the thought of Benny, she wondered what he was hiding. She turned on her radio, listening for any news of an earthquake. As she flipped from one country music station to the next, she finally gave up and turned it off.

With no distractions, her mind kept flashing to the angel captured momentarily on the tape. She was beautiful and sweet as she held the little girl's hand and looked up at her. Ethereal thoughts quickly gave way to concerns about what all of this meant. Was God trying to warn us to watch our step? Throughout time, psychics have predicted everything from assassinations to earthquakes to the end of the world. Few had paid attention. So why is it different now? She thought about the people she had interviewed who claimed they had not only seen, but had spoken to angels, and how they all seemed so believable.

Ellie LeBeaux instantly came to mind. But thoughts of Ellie brought her back to the church. Why would someone bomb Bethany Baptist Church? What could they possibly gain? Bethany Baptist was certainly the most vocal proponent of angel sightings. Was this a warning from someone? Ceaseless, unanswered questions kept coming to her as she sped back to New Orleans.

The sounds of soft jazz filtered through the Round Robin Bar inside the Willard Continental Bar in Washington DC as Mark Laux sipped his Irish coffee. Pete Vargas had called him that morning said he was on his way to a shoot at the White House, but wanted to meet with Mark around one o'clock. Mark quickly checked his watch for the third time. It was now twenty after. He took another sip and glanced around the dark paneled room. Two people sat on one side of the circular bar while a man on the other side, was in an animated discussion with the bartender over how to make a perfect mint julep. Otherwise, the bar was empty. Mark looked up and gave a wave as Pete came through the door with his camera bag hoisted over his shoulder.

"Sorry I'm late," he said as he sat across from Mark. "Had to do fifteen takes with Melanie. I think I've been spoiled working with Amanda. She's always been the one take lady."

"Yeah, I know," Mark said. "So, what's the big news?"

"I think I know who's behind WNN pulling the angel stories."

"Sure, I do, too," Mark said. "Fred Shelton told me ConTel and Minsinger didn't like the feedback they were getting from their customers."

"Well, that's the story they're handing out, but the real reason is their connection with the ACLU."

"The ACLU?" Mark asked surprised. "What do they have to do with it?"

"Apparently, both companies are quietly supporting them."

"That doesn't even make sense. I mean, why would these major companies risk alienating their customers by supporting an organization like that?"

"Basically, it's buying protection. If these companies throw money their way, they know the ACLU will leave them alone."

Mark looked at him uncertainly. "Where did you hear this?"

Pete smiled. "Hey man, I can't reveal my sources."

"Can it, Vargas. Who told you this?"

Pete laughed. "Hey, I've got a brother who works for ConTel and I asked him to nose around for me. Fortunately, he's dating the vice president's secretary."

"Well, that explains a lot," Mark said. "If the ACLU is dictating what's shown on the air, I wonder what else they're involved in."

It was just after 6:00 p.m. when Amanda finally returned to her hotel room. She immediately turned on the television to WNN. A commercial was on. She took off her coat and slung it over a chair and sat on the bed, waiting for the news program to resume. Melanie Sheldon was on with a report on terrorist activities that she had taped earlier at the

White House. Then Bob McNeill reported on sports with a wrap-up of the scores of the day and finally the weather. There was still no mention of an earthquake anywhere. She pulled out her cell phone and punched in Mark's number. He answered on the second ring.

"I've been trying to reach you," he said.

"When did you call?"

"A couple of hours ago."

"Oh well, that's not surprising. I've been off in the wild doing a little research. I went to Baton Rouge to check out the Spirit of Truth Church for myself. The good reverend wasn't there, but his slimy assistant was, and he obviously wasn't excited to see me. In fact, he couldn't wait to get rid of me."

"Did you find out anything?"

"No, he wouldn't even let me in the church. But April found something. Benny McDuff's last job before working at the church was at Louisiana State Prison, doing time for embezzlement. Interesting, huh? And, I'm not sure how, but she also found out that the Spirit of Truth accounts at several offshore banks have had huge deposits and withdrawals. My bet is that Reverend John and Benny are into money laundering. Just a guess, but the pieces are certainly coming together."

"Yeah, they are," Mark said. "And how convenient for Reverend John to hire someone who knows the ins and the outs of embezzling. Well, I have some news for you, too. I had a drink with our good friend Pete Vargas today. He found out why your stories were killed. Apparently, there's a connection between ConTel and Minsinger and the ACLU."

"What do they have to do with it?"

"It seems they pay the ACLU to keep them off their backs."

"The ACLU blackmails them?"

"Well, I don't think it's considered blackmail—more like greasing the palm, and if the ACLU doesn't like the programs these companies sponsor, they let them know it."

"And so, they basically censor the media. Wow," Amanda said. "I'm surprised I haven't run into this before."

"You probably have and just didn't know it."

"Unbelievable," Amanda whispered. "It's amazing, isn't it, how the public has no clue what's going on behind the scenes? I think if I were God, I wouldn't be too pleased with us either. By the way, I've been listening to the news all day and still haven't heard anything about an earthquake in Korea. Have you heard anything?"

"No, but the day isn't over yet."

CHAPTER TWENTY-TWO

It started with an almost indiscernible rumble—a small vibration that second-by-second built into a violent shaking. People began fleeing their crumbling homes. As they came out on to the streets, the undulating waves of the earth made standing impossible. Screams could be heard through the roar as the shaking continued, minute after eternal minute. Power lines fell on trees, igniting them into infernos. Gas lines exploded. Off in the distance, a church bell was furiously ringing. Ding, ding; ding, dong, ding; dong, ding.

Amanda woke with a start. Her heart was beating wildly as she heard the ringing of her cell phone. She took a deep breath to steady herself before answering. "Amanda Fox," she said with a shaky voice.

"It's happened." Mark said. "By the sound of your voice, though, you probably already know it."

"What?" she asked, confused. "The earthquake?"

"Yes! Little Katie's earthquake! You okay?"

"Yeah," she said hoarsely. "I was up all night checking the news. I don't know when I finally dozed off, but I had this horrible nightmare about an earthquake. I can still hear the screams. It was terrible." She paused a moment. "When did it happen?"

"Turn on the news." She punched the remote that was set on WNN. Karl Davis was on the air.

"A 7.8 magnitude earthquake centered in Seoul, Korea at 5:01 p.m., just about two hours ago," he began. Amanda glanced at the clock beside the bed which read 3:58 a.m. "We're just getting word on some of the damage. We have Ron Freeman standing by at YTV in Seoul."

"Karl, the scene around me is absolutely devastating. This massive earthquake, which has now been confirmed as an 8.1, has almost leveled Seoul. The JW Marriott, across the street from where I'm standing, is totally destroyed, as are most of the buildings in this area. This could not have happened at a worse time of day, since many people who were heading home from work are now trapped in the multitude of subways under this city.

We also had a report that two commuter trains have jumped the tracks and have crashed. Fires have broken out in several areas of the city, but because the streets are impassible at the moment, it's almost impossible to get the equipment in to put these fires out."

The ground began to shake again and Ron grabbed on to a nearby light pole. As he continued, the feed became scratchy. "We've…had… several of these…aftershocks and …" The television went to black.

The camera was back on Karl. "Apparently, we've lost the connection with Ron, but as we work to get it back, let me update you with a report I just received. Although it's early, the estimated death toll from this quake might surpass thirty thousand people."

Amanda clicked off the television and sat on the end of her bed. "She was right," she said with quiet emphasis. "Katie was right. Thirty thousand people, my God."

"And the next one will be New York," Mark said.

"Mark," she said raising her voice. "We've got to warn them. I've got to get back on the air."

"I know."

"I'll be on the first flight out," she said, holding the phone with one hand and grabbing her suitcase with the other.

"No, stay there. I think the best plan is to have Pete and me come to New Orleans."

"Why?"

"I'll explain when I get there. Try to get some sleep if you can."

"Sleeping's for amateurs," she said quietly. "See you soon." She clicked off her cell phone and laid back on the bed. Thoughts of her dream, of the earthquake, and of warning New York haunted, and finally exhausted her. Within minutes, she fell back to sleep.

At 8:45 a.m. Amanda had just emerged from the shower after a good four-hour sleep. She threw on a hotel robe and had begun to apply make-up when her cell phone rang.

"Ms. Fox? This is James Thomas."

"Good morning."

"I hope I'm not calling too early."

"No, it's fine. How can I help you?"

"Would it be possible for you to come to the church this morning?"

"Yes, of course," she said, with a note of curiosity in her voice. "Is this about the earthquake in Korea?"

"Not directly, but there is a matter that you need to know about. Would you be able to come around nine thirty?"

"I'll be there," she said as she checked her watch.

"Good. Thank you, Ms. Fox, I'll see you then."

At 9:29, Amanda walked into the church office and was surprised to see Ellie LeBeaux there. She extended her hand, "Ellie, delighted to see you again."

"Good morning, Ms. Fox."

Pastor Thomas emerged from his office when he heard Amanda's voice. "Thank you again for coming," he said, shaking her hand. "Please, come into my office." He escorted them in and closed the door. As they took their seats, he slipped into his leather chair.

"Your office looks so much better than it did yesterday," Amanda said as she saw everything back in its place.

He smiled. "We had a good team in here helping." He glanced at Ellie and clasped his hands together on his desk before continuing. He turned back to Amanda. "Ms. Fox, I've asked you to come here this morning because there has been another sighting."

Amanda turned to Ellie. "You've seen another angel?"

"Yes."

"When?"

"This morning. I was at home and I had just put a kettle on to boil when I turned around and saw a little boy sitting at my table. I was more than surprised and when I asked who he was, he told me he was an angel sent from God. He said he wanted me to deliver a second message."

Amanda shot a quick glance at Pastor Thomas and saw the concern in his eyes.

Ellie continued, "He said to tell the people that the children of God have defied His laws. They have hurt the smallest among them. They have lost reverence for Him and for their brothers and sisters. He wants you to tell the people to prepare themselves, for the time of God is at hand. The boy came over to me and said, 'Be strong,' then he touched my cheek, and then he vanished."

A chill ran through Amanda as she sat in stunned silence.

"Miss Ellie called me immediately after it happened."

A wave of fear swept through Amanda and her breathing became heavier as she pondered the implications.

"The time is at hand," Amanda whispered softly as she watched the leaves outside the window softly fluttering in the breeze. She looked back at Pastor Thomas. "Is this it then? Is this the end?"

Leaning toward her, in a very controlled voice, he said, "Only God can answer that question, Ms. Fox. As a student of the Bible, this was not what I expected, but who are we to second-guess God? It's odd, but even with such a frightening message, I somehow have this sense of calm. Perhaps it's my perception. I have always seen God as good, kind, and loving."

Amanda looked at him and wondered about a good, kind, and loving God who would let thirty thousand die in this morning's earthquake. She couldn't hold it in. She needed some answers. "Do you still see God as good, even with the earthquake this morning? So many people, so many children died."

"I know," he said quietly, "I wish I had the answers you want to hear, but I can only go with my core belief that He is good and He has his own reasons for all things that happen."

Ellie reached out and put her hand on Amanda's. "I've had my own doubts, too," she said softly. "When I lost my babies, I knew my heart would break. I felt so alone, even though I had my wonderful family and friends around me. Still," she said with measured words and continued, "the emptiness was there, and I wondered why God would cause such pain. It took me a while to realize that Pastor Thomas is right, that God has His own reasons for things to happen. Most of us see things only from our point of view. God, though, sees things in a much bigger sense. As I've lived these many years, I have come to understand how connected we all are and when we look back, we can often see why things happened the way they did. Perhaps, because of my pain, my faith has become even stronger." She gave Amanda a slight smile. "God is good, Ms. Fox. I know that."

Despite the reassuring words from Ellie, Amanda's mind was still spinning when she returned to the hotel. A major battle between belief and denial was raging within her. She turned the television on for distraction, keeping the volume low, and saw scenes of total destruction everywhere in Korea. Just then, the report switched to China. She turned up the volume.

"...in Qingdao, on the eastern edge of China sweeping people, animals and buildings out to sea. Qingdao sits on the Yellow Sea directly across from Seoul where the devastating earthquake occurred earlier. At this point we have no information on the loss of life..."

Katie had said a wall of water would hit China. Amanda thought of New York and knew the people had to be warned. Suddenly, she wondered why? What difference would it make to warn people if the world was going to end anyway? As quickly as the thought came, she banished it, chastising herself for giving up so easily. One way or another, she would get the message to them so they could save themselves. The little girl's words of 'those who believe will be saved' kept haunting her. As she continued to watch the earthquake coverage, she switched to ABC to see what slant they were giving the story. The reporter was interviewing a young man.

"And you say this woman, this angel, approached you this morning?"

"Yes, she was beautiful. She told me God has a message for the world. I wrote it out," the young man said it a shaky voice. "My children, you have defied my laws. You have hurt the smallest amongst you. You have lost reverence for me and for your brothers. Prepare yourselves. The time is at hand."

Amanda caught her breath. This was the exact message that Ellie had received.

The reporter continued, "When did this happen?"

"Early this morning. I was jogging, and then I saw her."

"What do you think the message means?"

"I don't...I don't know. I just... She was beautiful...and then she just disappeared."

The reporter turned to the camera. "We've been getting these same reports from all over the world; the same message, happening all at the same time. From what I've been able to gather from my sources, it's possible that this is yet another terrorist tactic to spread fear throughout the world. The president this morning has asked the FBI to investigate. This is George Kelly, ABC News."

Amanda's tension gave way, and she almost laughed at the ridiculousness of the situation. So now the FBI is going to investigate God? Her cell phone rang, and she saw that it was Mark. "Hi, are you here already?"

"Change of plans. You've seen the latest reports?"

"Yes, in fact, Pastor Thomas called me this morning. Ellie LeBeaux has had another angel encounter. In fact, the message she told me this morning was word-for-word what I just saw on ABC. I don't even know what to think about all of this." She stopped for a moment. "What do you mean, a change of plans? What's going on?"

"I had a phone call from Martin Scolesco. He wants us back. The other networks are getting all the press and he's not happy about it. Catch the first plane you can and plan on doing your show tonight. I'll start scripting here and you add the conversation with Pastor Thomas.

And Amanda," he added with quiet emphasis, "New York will be warned."

Amanda was quiet.

"Still there?"

"Yeah," she whispered. "This is all so unbelievable. I'm really scared, Mark. What's the point of warning everyone if we're all going to die anyway?"

"None of us was preordained to live forever, Amanda. We all have our time to die—some of us earlier, like my wife and son." He paused before continuing, "After they died, I almost felt like giving up myself, but deep inside, I knew that was wrong. It isn't the amount of time you have on this earth; it's what you do with that time. As Pollyanna as it sounds, I originally became a reporter so that I could help as many people as I could with honest reporting. If we all die tomorrow and I've been able to make a difference along the way, I feel that my life was worth something."

From the beginning, Amanda knew there was something special about Mark, and now he had finally vocalized it. Feeling momentarily ashamed of her own weakness, she forced herself to calm down. "You really are incredible, you know," she said softly. Then, with a strength that surprised even her, "I'll get my notes together on the plane and see you soon."

CHAPTER TWENTY-THREE

P alm fronds rustled overhead and the evocative scent of coconut oil filled the air as the warm Florida breeze caressed every part of Reverend John Winter's body. The masseuse was particularly good today, artfully massaging every hill and valley of his massive bulk as soothing tones of Diana Krall's "Peel Me a Grape" softly emanated from discreetly hidden speakers beside his swimming pool.

His normal massage time was one hour, but the day was so perfect he extended that by a half-hour, not wishing the deliciously sensual feelings to end. When at last he was satiated and the masseuse had left, he slowly eased himself off the table and walked to the pool.

The sun glistened off all parts of his oiled body. Walking down the steps, he gently lowered himself into the warm water and slowly swam the length of the pool. After two more laps, he went back up the steps and walked over to the table, where he wrapped himself in his robe. He glanced up at his new home and smiled with satisfaction.

The twelve thousand square foot Mediterranean-style mansion was better than he hoped it would be. It was now his new favorite among all of his homes. From its polished marble floors to its sweeping staircase, grandeur was the only way to describe this Italianate-style palazzo. Baccarat crystal chandeliers hung throughout the home, with the most spectacular one in the dining room gracefully shimmering over the ten-foot-ong mahogany table.

His favorite area of the house, though, was the master bedroom suite. It encompassed three rooms which included the main bedroom, a twenty-foot sitting room with fireplace, and the marble covered bath with a sauna, king-sized whirlpool bathtub, steam shower, and an exercise room. The master suite alone took up almost twenty-five hundred square feet.

His thoughts were interrupted when Kingston, the live-in butler, or 'gentleman's gentleman', as he preferred being called, approached him. Tall, dark haired, and British, James Kingston was the quintessential valet. He actually came with the home. When the previous owner died, Reverend John asked Kingston if he would stay on, and he happily accepted.

"Sir, I have a call for you on line one from a Mr. McDuff."

"Thanks, Kingston. I'll take it in the pavilion." He slipped into his sandals and pulled his robe tighter as he made his way toward the pavilion on the other side of the pool. As he entered the open-air room, a breeze caught the sheer drapes, swirling them around him. He went to the bar, poured himself a whiskey, and heavily sat down in a huge rattan chair. After propping his feet on the ottoman, he lifted the receiver and punched line one. "Benny, are you already in New York?"

"Yeah, just checked into the St. Regis. We've got the presidential suite. Everything's all ready for you."

"Great, great," Reverend John said as he took a sip of his drink. "Dave has the plane warmed up and ready and I'll be at the airport in about an hour. It's not going to be easy leaving, though. You should see this place, Benny." He paused for a second, and took another drink. "It's better than fabulous. Well worth fund-raising," he said with a laugh.

"Yeah, well, while you're sitting there in the lap of luxury, we had a visitor. That snoopy reporter came to the church yesterday. I caught her nosing around in the back."

Reverend John's good humor quickly evaporated. "Amanda Fox? What did she want?"

"She said she was in New Orleans and just wanted to stop by for a neighborly visit."

"Right," he murmured satirically.

"She even wanted to come in and look around, but I blew her off. I don't trust that broad. I just know she's trying to get something on us."

Reverend John leaned back and crossed his ankles. "What could she find, Benny? Outwardly, everything's on the up and up."

"Yeah, but think about it. She's down in New Orleans, probably chatting it up with that black pastor who told her all about his run-in with you in the early days. He's filled her head with all kinds of things and now she's trying to dig up some dirt."

Reverend John laughed, "Well, there's plenty of dirt to find, but stop worrying, Benny. You've covered everything. There's nothing directly in my name anywhere."

He took another long drink. "So, how are the ticket sales coming in New York?"

"Well, there's the good news. We're sold out for the dinner tomorrow night. At a thousand dollars a plate, we're going to clear around six hundred thousand."

"Great. How about Friday's show?"

"Sold out—even a wait list. I heard scalpers are getting as much as one hundred a ticket, but hey, we're going to end up with about a million ourselves."

"See? I told you not to worry. We're invincible and it's only getting better. It's going to be fine. I'll see you at the St. Regis in a few hours."

He hung up and took another long drink as he contemplated all the money he was making. Then, as the warm breeze caressed his skin, he smiled—convinced, once again, that this gravy train showed no sign of stopping.

CHAPTER TWENTY-FOUR

"Hey, welcome back," April said as she saw Amanda approach her desk. "I saw your show. Geez, this thing is so scary." She paused a moment as she studied Amanda. "Do you really think New York will have an earthquake on Friday?"

Amanda shook her head. "I don't know. I think so, but I don't know. I can only repeat what the little girl told me, and she was right about Korea."

"My mom lives in New York," April said, obviously worried. "I'm not sure how I'm going to convince her to leave, especially when she sees this." She turned around a copy of the New York Times with the headline, 'Terrorists Breed Fear into New Yorkers with Tale of Earthquake.' The article went on to say that the chance of an earthquake in New York was close to zero. The mayor was quoted as saying, "New Yorkers will never cower to these terrorists. Be strong and go on about your daily lives."

Amanda let out an audible breath. "I know, I saw it all on the news this morning. They've convoluted the whole thing."

April looked up at Amanda. "What should I do? Think she'd be safe upstate?"

"The little girl wasn't any more specific than New York. That could include upstate. Why don't you have her come visit for a few days?"

"I don't know. She'll never leave her dog."

"Dogs ride on airplanes, too, April. Best to be safe."

April smiled. "You're right."

As Amanda turned to walk back to her office, April called her back. "By the way, I have more information on Reverend John." She opened her file door and pulled out a folder. "The Spirit of Truth Church has had extremely large withdrawals, all made out to the same name, the Thomas Sheldon Foundation. I checked and there is no such foundation, so I went a step further and traced those deposits to the Children of Mercy Account at another bank in the Caymans. Then it goes to a private Swiss bank account."

Amanda's eyebrows shot up. "How on earth did you find all of this?"

"Don't ask," April said. "But it's all there—right down to account numbers. I'm so disgusted with this man I could spit, especially since I trusted him with my own money. My mom even donated to him because I told her how great he was."

"Well, thanks to you, we're going to expose him for the fraud that he is. Great job, April."

"Well, I'll sleep better knowing he's behind bars," April muttered.

Amanda walked into her office and slid the folder with Reverend John's information into a drawer. As much as she would like to see the good reverend get nailed, the situation in New York took precedence at the moment. She had warned them on her program last night, but how could she make them understand the danger they were in? Katie didn't specify whether the earthquake would hit New York City or elsewhere in the state, so what could anyone realistically do—evacuate the entire state?

A feeling of total helplessness came over her. People were going to die and there wasn't anything she could do about it. Her brother used to say, "Just let go and let God." For someone like herself, who needed to be in control all the time, it was almost impossible to just let go. Now, though, she knew she didn't have a choice.

CHAPTER TWENTY-FIVE

Friday morning at 4:14, the ringing of the phone woke Amanda.

"Ms. Fox? This is Win Jefferies with CNC. Just wanted to get your reaction to the earthquake in New York."

"What?"

"The earthquake that shook New York City about twenty minutes ago. You said that a little girl predicted this. What was the spelling on her name again? And what are her parents' names?"

Amanda, still groggy, punched the remote beside her bed and tried to focus on the screen. "Listen," she said, "I'll have to have to get back to you." She hung up and immediately called Mark.

"Mark. It's happened. Turn on the TV."

"I know. I just had a call from a friend at the Times and as he was telling me about it, the line went dead."

"This is incredible," she said as she watched the jumble of buildings piled in the street. Smoke was rising and people were fleeing, not even certain where to go. An aftershock sent more debris down on the street, crushing cars and people. "I tried to tell them," she said to herself as she watched the devastation.

"I know you did," Mark said quietly. "You did all you could. It was their decision to stay." "Would you like me to come over?" Mark asked.

"Yeah," she whispered. "I really would." She quickly showered, changed, and had coffee on by the time Mark rang the doorbell. She opened the door and couldn't restrain herself as she reached out for him. Life was becoming more and more frightening and she just needed to be held. After a moment, she pulled back and looked into his eyes, and gave him a sad smile.

"You okay?" he asked, still holding her.

"Yeah, much better—now that you're here." The sound of the television blared in the background. The cell phone rang again. "Come on in and help yourself to some coffee," she said as she went to answer it. She clicked on the phone. "Amanda Fox."

"Amanda, it's Jay. Sorry to call you so early, but I'm sure you know what's happening in New York. Our whole show is going to be dedicated to the earthquake today, and I'd like you to come on."

Amanda took a deep breath. "Yeah, I can do that. What time do you want me?"

"We'll do the segment about 1:15."

"Good, okay, I'll be there." She looked over at Mark, now sitting on the sofa sipping his coffee. "Jay Walters wants me to do a segment on the Jay Report today. I told him I would."

"Be prepared," Mark warned. "The onslaught is coming."

"I know," she said. "It's news, and that's what we do. How can I say no?" They refocused their attention on the television as they watched scene after scene of damaged buildings, buckled streets, and downed bridges. It seemed like something out of Hollywood, but this was real.

"Benny," yelled Reverend John as he raced as fast as he could through the debris of the presidential suite of the St. Regis Hotel. Dodging overturned furniture and broken glass, he stumbled through the living room and then past the dining room, slowly making his way to Benny McDuff's bedroom. "Benny," he yelled again.

In the distance, he heard a moan. He worked faster, shoving fallen art out of the way. When he finally reached the bedroom, he found Benny lying on the floor. A Waterford crystal chandelier had fallen from the fourteen-foot ceiling, piercing Benny's chest. Blood covered the white carpet.

"My God, Benny," he said, as he tried lifting the heavy chandelier from Benny's body. Finally, with strength he never realized he had, he managed to shove it off to the side, cutting himself on the spiky shards of crystal. He lifted Benny's head. "Benny, I'll get help. Hang on."

Benny's eyes opened, and he tried to focus on Reverend John. He coughed, and blood trickled down from the corner of his mouth. "Too…late," he said. "You'll…have to watch your back…on your own," he rasped.

An aftershock, almost as great as the first earthquake, sent furniture plummeting—once again rolling Reverend John into the shattered chandelier. Agonizing minutes went by as Limoges china crashed to the floor all around him. Finally, the shaking stopped. Through the eerie silence, John looked over at Benny and saw that he was gone. "No," he sobbed as he curled into a fetal position on the floor.

In the Hamptons, Andrew Melton moaned as he lay on the floor. The shaking of the earthquake was so severe, it had tossed him to the ground. The earthquake's force scattered debris everywhere. He tried to get up, but an excruciating pain shot through his arm and back. He tried calling for help, but was too weak. He was drenched in sweat.

Within minutes, Gerald, his butler, covered with dust and blood, rushed into his room and cleaned the debris off of his bed. "Sir," he said, "let me help." He carefully lifted him back into his bed. Andrew Melton could barely lift his head. Suddenly, he felt a wave of nausea and he threw up all over his Egyptian cotton sheets and his silk bedding. Another surge of nausea followed this, resulting in additional vomit that included blood.

Gerald rushed to the bathroom to get wet cloths to clean him. When he returned, he saw that Andrew Melton was trying to speak.

"The others," said weakly. "How are they?"

"Not well, I fear. I have sent both the maids and the butlers to assist," he said, wiping his boss's face. "The house is a shambles and the guest houses are destroyed."

Andrew Melton looked at Gerald and whispered, almost to himself. "The Alliance is gone." He watched as his valet tried to clean the bedding. He glanced at the shambles of his room, and took his final breath.

CHAPTER TWENTY-SIX

Jay Walters adjusted his microphone during the break and saw that Amanda had arrived early. He gave her a quick wave and waited as the floor director signaled five seconds to air.

"We're back, and joining us from New York is Mayor Christopher O'Brien. Thanks for being with us today, mayor. I know your schedule is extremely full, so we appreciate your time. Could you fill us in on the most recent information in New York? I understand that fires continue to burn out of control."

The mayor, wearing a soot-covered FDNY sweatshirt, held his earpiece in tighter to block out the sirens in the background as he looked at the camera. "Yes, as you can see in the background, smoke is covering the city and almost blacking out the sun. Many streets are impassible, and we ask all who are not emergency personnel to please stay off the streets that are open so that first responders can get through."

"I have heard that the airports have suffered damage as well. Can you confirm that?"

"Yes, Newark, LaGuardia, and JFK have all suffered major damage, both in the terminals and on the roads and runways. Several runways are buckled, and all of these airports have been shut down.

We're working on the problem now, but I feel it will be some time before these airports are operational again."

"We had an earlier report that part of the Empire State Building had sustained damage. Is that correct?"

"Yes, the north side façade has collapsed. We have rescue teams there and at the Metropolitan Museum of Art."

"Mayor, have you any idea of the casualties yet?"

"No," the mayor said somberly. "We've had estimates of between ten and twenty thousand, but there's no way to tell at this stage. We have triage sites set up at various places in the city. We've reserved the hospitals for level one patients who are the most critical. Many schools and libraries are taking in patients for levels two and three, which includes broken bones and non-life-threatening injuries. In Central Park, as well as other parks throughout the city, we've set up tents for levels four and five, which includes minor injuries. These tents are also places to receive bottled water and food."

"We're showing a list of all the locations for the various levels on the screen right now, mayor. We know you're busy, but thank you for taking time to be with us today."

"Thank you, Jay," the mayor said and quickly turned off-camera to confer with the fire chief.

"A devastating situation in New York right now," Jay said to his viewers. "It's hard to even imagine. Cathy Sandoz is on satellite feed from New York right now." He turned to the monitor. "Cathy, what can you tell us about ongoing rescue efforts?"

"Jay, I'm standing in front of what is left of the Metropolitan Museum of Art. Rescue teams are out in full force all through the city. Policemen, firemen, rescue dogs, and volunteers are searching building by building for survivors. The search is difficult since the power is out in many parts of the city and many streets are impassable.

"The Federal Disaster Recovery Agency has already arrived on scene with food, water, and supplies. This new FDR Agency needs to be commended for its efficiency. It's a far cry from the FEMA days." A policeman came up to Cathy and spoke to her, and she nodded. "Jay, we've been asked to clear away from the front of this building since an aftershock could send more rubble tumbling down onto the street."

"Thanks, Cathy. Keep yourself safe." Jay turned back toward the camera. "As the world watches, many people are becoming extremely concerned about what's been happening in our world today—especially in view of the fact that this earthquake was predicted by a little nine- year-old girl who claimed that an angel told her this would happen. We need to take a quick break, but when we return, Amanda Fox, who interviewed that little girl, will be joining us."

"And we're clear," the director said.

Jay stood up and extended his hand to Amanda. "Thanks for coming on the show."

"Incredible, isn't it?" she said, clasping his hand. He pulled out a chair for her.

"We'll have two other guests today on live feed. Dr. Elizabeth Margo from L.A. and Victoria Davis-Smith from Houston."

"I've seen Ms. Davis-Smith on other segments, but I've never met her."

"She's a real firecracker. That's why I have her on the show."

"It's never a dull time with you, Jay," she said with a smile.

"And five," the director said as he counted down.

"We're back with Amanda Fox in our studio, and joining us from Los Angeles, Dr. Margo Stein; from Houston, ACLU attorney Victoria Davis-Smith; and in Tehran, our reporter Wes Ross. Thank you all for being here today. Before we get started, let's go to the tape." They watched the monitor as Katie was telling Amanda about the prediction of the earthquakes.

"So little Katie has been right about two of the three earthquakes so far," Jay said to Amanda.

Amanda nodded. "Yes, it was quite an interview."

"And if she's right, the next one will be in Iran."

"That's what she said."

"Do you believe this is the end of the world?"

"Oh, come on," Victoria Davis-Smith interrupted, laughing. "This is what's wrong with the media today. These giant leaps. What are you trying to do, Jay, intentionally scare us all to death?"

Amanda ignored Victoria's interruption. "I don't know if this is the end of the world or not," she said, "but I do think that the majority of the people who claim to have seen these angels have been very believable."

"Let's go to Wes Ross in Tehran. Wes, what has been the reaction there to this earthquake and the prediction?"

There was a pause as Wes listened to the question. "Jay, people are nervous here. Earlier today on Al Jazeera TV, the Iranian president delivered a message to the people. Let me read the text. He said, 'Once again, Islam rules supreme. New York, lover of Israel, has been struck down by Allah himself and is burning in the fire of Allah's fury. All who recognize the Zionist regime will burn as well. With their city on its knees, the American infidels are now trying to frighten us with their terrorist fears, stating that their God will send an earthquake to Iran. We will not cower to their lies. Recognize who your enemy is.'

"I spoke to Shiek Abd Al-Sali, a Sunni cleric, today," Ross contin-ued. "He said a fatwa has been issued, proclaiming that anyone who believes the infidels will be branded an infidel himself and will be punished. He said Allah will protect Iran and that the truth will be revealed as a pack of Western lies only to spread fear." The screen began to show static as he continued his report. "Al Jazeera has been reporting…Christian lies…Jihad…"

Jay looked at the camera. "Our apologies, ladies and gentlemen. We seem to have lost the signal. As we try to get Wes back, let's go to you, Dr. Margo. What do you think is going on with the angel sightings and these predictions? Is this the end of the world?"

"Yes, I think it is—or at least the world as we know it," she said emphatically. "We seem to have lost a moral framework in our world. Personally, I think God's fed up."

"You think that God, being an all forgiving and all loving God, can get fed up?" Jay asked.

"Yes, I do," she said. "Not unlike a parent with a spoiled child who finally says, 'enough is enough.'"

"Yes, but we're talking about the destruction of cities and the deaths of multitudes of people."

"Well, if you've read the Bible, He's done it before. Remember Sodom and Gomorrah? And how about the flood?"

"Myths," interrupted Victoria.

"You don't believe?" Jay asked.

"I believe the Bible has a certain history, but I think most of it was put in there to make people behave the way the good church leaders wanted them to. It's a control thing. Religious leaders are still trying to do it today."

"What about angel sightings and the prediction of the earthquakes?"

"These supposed angel sightings have simply been mass hysteria, which I still say, Jay, is because of media coverage. Most of which, I might add, has been aired on WNN. The Iranians at least are recognizing this."

"How about the earthquake predictions? The little girl was right about two out of three so far."

"I think certain people have psychic abilities. I'm sure she's one of them. But even the best psychics can be wrong, too."

"So God's not involved?" Jay asked.

"God, or whatever passes for God, is not," Victoria said firmly.

"With all due respect," Dr. Margo interjected, "I think Ms. Davis-Smith seems to be talking in circles. The word psychic is derived from the Greek word psuhikos, which means 'of the soul.' Now, if the belief is that we have souls, which historically is our connection to divinity, and the soul continues after life is over, then the little girl certainly has a connection to God."

Victoria shot back, "The good doctor is not the only one who paid attention in English 101. Soul, literally translated, also means 'returning to the sea,' which also means that Darwin was right. God didn't create man. We simply evolved from the sea."

Jay interrupted her and turned to Amanda, "You've spoken with several people now who have claimed to see angels. What do you really think is going on?"

Amanda looked at Jay. "Before the sightings, I might have agreed with Ms. Davis-Smith, but after speaking with these people, who are so believable, I would say there's something happening that's much larger than we are."

"Are you saying this is the end of the world?"

"I don't know, but I do feel that this definitely is a wake-up call."

Just as Victoria Davis-Smith began to protest, Jay held up his hand. "Looks like we're going to have it leave it here. We're all out of time. Thanks to all my guests." He pointed to the camera. "And you, dear friends, have been watching the Jay Report. See you tomorrow with our guest, Senator Joe Rapini from New York."

"We're clear," the director said.

"Good show," Jay said as he unhooked his microphone.

"Too bad you lost that connection with Wes," Amanda said.

"Yeah, I know. Interesting, the Islamic slant on these earthquakes, isn't it?"

"Well, I don't wish an earthquake on anybody, but I really think chances are that it's going to happen. I mean, who would ever think it would happen in New York? I didn't even think they had fault lines, but Katie was right about that. I think she'll be right again."

CHAPTER TWENTY-SEVEN

The heavy smell of alcohol permeated the air and moans echoed through the gymnasium where dozens of cots were laid out side by side in neat rows. Nurses and nuns were scurrying about attending the injured as two doctors on duty were kept busy setting broken bones and assessing the wounds inflicted by the earthquake.

"Doctor," shouted one of the nurses, "convulsions." The patient was writhing in pain. The nurse tried to hold him down as his twisting and turning turned to violent shaking.

"This patient is level one," the doctor said, readying a needle. "Let's get him stabilized and out of here. He needs to be sent to a hospital now." He turned to another nurse who was coming toward them. "Come over here and help hold this patient down," he ordered. Between the two of them, the doctor was finally able to administer the shot. Within seconds a gurney appeared and the patient was wheeled out of the room.

The commotion instantly awakened Reverend John. Still dazed, with a slight head injury, he looked around the immense room lined wall to wall with cots. Where in the hell am I?, he wondered. He tried to sit up but instantly fell back as a searing pain shot through his head. From his vantage point he could see a nun passing by, and he reached out and grabbed her skirt. She stopped and turned to him. He tried to focus on her. "Where am I?" he whispered hoarsely.

She gently loosened his grip and took his hand in hers. "You are at the Convent of the Sacred Heart School. You were brought here last night. Do you remember the earthquake?"

The earthquake, he thought. Oh, God. The nightmare rushed over him again with the realization that Benny had been killed. How could he manage his finances without him? He turned away from the nun as tears flowed down his cheeks.

"Are you in pain?"

"My head," he said, trying to move his feet. "I can't move," he said. "My feet, I can't move my feet."

"Your right leg is broken and it's in a cast," she said gently. "Your left leg is fine, but we thought it would be best to strap you down so you wouldn't injure yourself."

"I have to get out of here," he said. As he tried once again to rise, the nun gently pushed his shoulders back down toward the pillow. "You need to rest," she said.

"But I need to get back to Baton Rouge. My doctor is there," he whispered. "Where is my cell phone? I need my cell phone."

"I'm sorry. I didn't see a phone. You really need to rest. Let me get you something to help with your headache," she said as she tucked his blanket around him.

Reverend John's eyes flashed wildly. "Do you know who I am?"

She adjusted the bandages on his head. "You were brought in without identification," she said gently. "Are you having trouble remembering?"

His expression clouded with anger. "Good God, woman," he yelled, "I'm Reverend John Winters. Don't you ever watch TV?"

"Mr. Winters," she ordered in a voice of authority, "it's not good for you to get so excited."

"Reverend John," he yelled, sending yet another surge of pain through his head.

"You're going to have to calm down," she said firmly. "You're disturbing the other patients." She quickly looked around, searching for assistance. "Doctor," she called. As the doctor came over and prepared a sedative, Reverend John turned his head away. His mind raced wildly —Benny's dead; I'm being held here against my will, strapped down like an animal. No cell phone, no credit cards. He felt the sting of the needle in his arm. The last thought he had, as he drifted off to sleep, was wondering if hell could be any worse.

CHAPTER TWENTY-EIGHT

"Amanda, you have a visitor. He said he wanted to surprise you." Amanda looked through the window toward April's desk and saw her brother, David. She raced out of the room.

"David," she said as she hugged him, "what are you doing here?"

"Amanda," he said, looking into her eyes, "it's so good to see you."

"Come on in," she said as she linked his arm and escorted him into her office. "Can I get you some coffee?"

He smiled and sat down in a chair across from her. "No, I'm fine."

"So, what brings you here?"

"Actually, the Vatican has sent me here to see you." His Holiness is coming for a U.S. visit. He will be in Baltimore tomorrow and he has requested to have a meeting with you."

She was astonished. "With me? Why?"

David smiled. "I'm only the messenger."

She thought back to the brief time she spent with Cardinal Martinelli, now Pope James, and remembered what a remarkable man he was. "Where would he like to have this meeting?"

"At ten a.m. at the Cathedral of Mary our Queen, the same church that Pope John Paul II visited on his last trip to Baltimore. If you are able to make this meeting, he asked that I escort you there."

"Of course I'll be there," she replied, still astonished that the pope wanted to see her. "I'm just overwhelmed." She looked at David, her younger brother, now resplendent in his clerical collar. "You look great. I'm so glad you're here. How long can you stay?"

"Just one night I'm afraid. I have meetings scheduled tomorrow afternoon in Baltimore and then I'll be returning to Portland on the six o'clock flight."

She smiled. "In time for early mass on Sunday." He nodded and returned her smile. "Then let's not waste a minute," she said as she quickly checked her watch. "Have you eaten? Are you hungry?"

"Actually, yes. I skipped lunch."

"Okay then, how about an early dinner?" She picked up the phone and punched in April's number. "I'm heading off. Catch me on my cell if you need me."

Even at this early hour, the Capital Grill was already filled with delicious aromas. Fortunately, it was was also quiet at this time of day. The earliest dinner reservations usually began around eight, so Amanda and David were able to talk without the commotion of the crowd.

"So, how are you?" Amanda asked as she unfolded her napkin and placed it on her lap. Before he had a chance to answer, she added, "I guess I don't have to ask that. With a special request of the Pope and meetings in Baltimore, you must be doing very well."

He smiled. "I think His Holiness was more interested in seeing you and because I had already been scheduled for meetings in Baltimore, I think they thought that I was your logical escort."

"I interviewed him in Rome. Did you see the tape?"

"Yes, it was a wonderful interview. I was so proud of you."

She smiled. "It was luck, pure and simple."

"Well, more like divine providence, I think," he replied as he took a sip of water.

She looked at him with somber curiosity. "Why did you do it, David? Why did you become a priest?"

He smiled, "Well, I guess you could say I was called."

"Called? What does that mean, called?"

"Well, in my case, it was this overwhelming feeling, almost a tugging at my soul. As much as I tried to ignore it, the feeling just wouldn't go away. Dad questioned me, my friends tried to talk me out of it, and I even remember you being very upset with my decision. Even so, it just seemed like a right move for me."

"Has it been?"

"Yes," he replied with certainty, and then was thoughtful for a moment. "It hasn't been an easy road, but nothing worthwhile ever is."

"It's funny, isn't it? We're like polar opposites. You've immersed yourself in the spiritual world and my world is based in secularism. Unfortunately, it's sensational news that sells, whether it's war or child abductions or killings. Heavens knows, in this world today, there's no end to the stories. It's enough to turn anyone into a cynic."

He looked into her eyes questioningly. "So why do you stay?"

She shrugged slightly. "I don't know. At first, I thought fame and glory were wonderful, but after a while it just didn't seem quite as important. I've never really thought about why I've stayed other than being a reporter is something I know, but if I were to pinpoint it, I suppose I'd have to say that I'd like to make a difference in people's lives." She laughed and shook her head. "Sounds kind of simplistic, doesn't it?"

"No," he said, "it sounds positive and you are doing it, you know, with your reports of angel sightings, for instance."

She looked into his eyes. "You've seen the reports?"

"Of course."

"These people have been very believable, but even so, I wasn't sure if the whole thing was a publicity stunt or something else until I actually saw an angel myself."

His eyebrows shot up. "You saw an angel?"

"Yes, but not the way the others had. This was a child angel that we caught on tape. Did you see the interview of the little girl who predicted the earthquakes?"

He nodded.

"When they first played the tape, they saw an angel sitting between me and the little girl. When they replayed it, my producer and I saw her as well."

He looked confused. "I didn't see an angel."

"No, when we aired the tape, she was gone. There was nothing but a blur."

"Do you think someone tampered with the tape to play a joke on you?"

"Now who's being the cynic? No, no one tampered with the tape. I don't know why she was there and then disappeared." Her voice drifted off to a hushed whisper. "I don't know why any of this is happening. End times? I don't know. I'm thinking about it again and again. I have to say, though, with all the misery in the world today, I can't blame God for getting fed up."

"God is a God of love. God doesn't get fed up."

She turned her head slightly and looked at him out of the corner of her eye. "Tell that to Noah."

CHAPTER TWENTY-NINE

A chilling autumn breeze sent a flurry of orange and yellow leaves through the air as Amanda and David approached the Cathedral of Mary our Queen in Baltimore. The church, with its gleaming limestone exterior, was a massive 343 feet long and had a roofline that soared ninety feet into the air. Twin towers that stood 160 feet high flanked the entry. Two gentlemen wearing dark suits and dark glasses checked their identification and held the Narthex doors open for them.

Monsignor McKnight was in a discussion with two other priests when he noticed Amanda and David. He turned and came toward them with his hand extended. "Ms. Fox, welcome to our parish."

"Thank you."

He turned toward David. "And Father, thank you so much for your assistance. His Holiness is waiting for you in the small conference room. I'll escort you there."

They followed him along the limestone floors past the sanctuary, where Amanda caught a quick glimpse of the Gothic arches and predominantly blue stained-glass windows of the magnificent interior. They continued on to a staircase where they ascended three floors. Finally, Monsignor McKnight held the door opened for them as they entered the ornate conference room. Pope James was seated on a special chair flown in from Italy. He was speaking to a small group of people. A priest went over and whispered in his ear, and he nodded. He spoke softly to the people, and they each kissed his ring and quietly left the room.

Monsignor McKnight kneeled and kissed his ring. "Your Holiness, Amanda Fox and Father David are here at your request." After the formalities, Monsignor McKnight took his leave and the three of them were alone in the room.

"Ms. Fox," the pope began. "I'm so very glad to see you again. I want to thank you for keeping your part of the bargain when you interviewed me in Rome." His eyes twinkled. "It doesn't always happen with reporters."

Amanda smiled.

"Your reports of angel sightings have come to my attention," he continued with a more serious tone in his voice. "I would like you to tell me what you know about these and what you believe to be true." He sat back in his chair and waited.

"Your Holiness," Amanda said after a moment, "I believe that God has sent angels to warn us." She recounted the stories—from the woman in Rome to the prisoner in Peru to the little girl in Canada—and finally to the multiple sightings where each person recited the same message from God.

"The little girl in Canada was right about the first two earthquakes. When our cameraman brought the footage back to the studio..." She hesitated, trying to find the right words.

"Yes?"

David glanced quickly at Amanda. "Several of us actually saw an angel on the tape sitting between the girl and me," she continued. "But when we showed it on the air that night, there was only a blur."

The pope crossed his fingers against his chest and leaned forward, his face creased with worry. "And the child said the next earthquake would be in Iran in three more days?"

"Yes," Amanda whispered. "Three days from yesterday's earthquake in New York."

The pope nodded, deep in thought. Amanda looked at Pope James and noticed a change in him since she had last seen him in Rome. Now, it seemed that his whole countenance was heavier. His brows drew together in an agonized expression and his eyes, although warm and kind, held an inexplicable sadness. She thought of Pope John Paul II, who was such a vibrant pope and who, through the years, had grown old before his time. The burdens of office were definitely evident in Pope James.

"Your Holiness," Amanda ventured as she looked into his eyes, "are these the end times? Is this the end of the world?"

He was quiet for a moment and then said, "Only God can answer that question, Ms. Fox. My personal feeling," he continued slowly, "is that mankind is increasingly causing God much sorrow. We're living in a very difficult world right now due in no small measure to our selfishness. Children disrespect authority. Nations and religions disrespect each other and that leads to war and suffering and killing. Not unlike Sodom and Gomorrah, what God has created, He can also destroy."

A chill, black silence fell over the room as the pope paused to gather his thoughts. Both Amanda's and David's eyes were riveted on him as they waited. Fear knotted up inside Amanda with the enormous reality that the end of the world could very well be eminent. She glanced quickly at David who appeared steady, but pale.

"My children," the pope continued, "I believe that God is a most merciful God. I also believe that He answers prayers, and I believe that the only thing that will save us will be our faith. Pray for your brothers and sisters on this earth. Pray for peace. Pray for the world." He gave each of them a blessing, and within a moment, a priest entered the room to escort them out of the building.

"Come back home soon, Amanda" David said as he walked her to her car. "You need to be with Dad. We need to be with you, especially now." Deep worry-lines were evident on his face.

"I promise I will just as soon as I can. Right now I'm needed here, just as you're needed there," she said. She gave him a warm hug, then stepped back and looked into his eyes. "I don't know what's happening, David, but I do know that I love you and I'm so proud of you. Take care of Dad and send him my love."

"I will and you'll be in our prayers," he said with a faint smile, "as you always have been."

"I know," she said, "I've felt it."

CHAPTER THIRTY

Saturday morning a cold rain was falling in New York, hindering the earthquake clean-up efforts. Streets were still littered with concrete and steel from the buckled buildings, and broken glass was everywhere. New York's finest were on the job, protecting what was left of the merchandise in the stores. Looters had zoomed into the city, like bees to honey, within an hour of the earthquake. Since the streets were impassible, most of the goods were carried away in the arms of the looters, although some entrepreneurial souls found wheelbarrows and loaded them full.

Emergency rescue efforts were still going on in several areas of the city, including the collapsed subways. Thousands still remained trapped inside. Many buildings were so unstable that rescue workers put themselves in extreme danger just going inside, especially because hundreds of aftershocks continued to plague the city.

The earthquake had crushed the Chrysler Building from seventy-seven to forty-eight stories, and rescue workers had to plucked victims from the top floors one at a time using a crane. Trump World Tower fared better, due to the fact that it was a newer building. Those who had survived, and who were able to walk down the seventy-two floors of the building, managed to escape through the front door.

Rescue dogs were still sniffing the debris at the Empire State Building, cutting their paws on shards of glass in their attempt to locate victims. Utility personnel working around the clock had restored power in many parts of the city. Despite their efforts, some 480,000 people were still in the dark.

At the Convent of the Sacred Heart, the power had been on for almost a full day. Reverend John awoke again from his drug-induced sleep and squinted at the brightness of the lights. He was surprisingly comfortable at the moment, due to the fact that he was absolutely still.

He was no longer restrained, since he learned quickly that any movement caused pain. So he lay on his cot calmly, watching the nurses and doctors race by. He felt a movement on his face as a trickle of blood slowly rolled down from his forehead, but he tried to ignore it. For the first time in his life, he had a thought about Jesus and his crown of thorns. He quickly dismissed it—thinking that this Catholic atmosphere must be the reason.

"Oh, Reverend Winters," Sister Margaret said as she came over to him. Reverend John, he thought, Reverend John, but he said nothing to her. He was sick to death of the blasted shots and wanted what was left of his wits about him, so he was quiet. "We need to change those bandages," she said, "I'll be right back with fresh ones." No, he thought, don't move me. God above, I'm finally comfortable.

She was back within a moment and began removing the blood-soaked gauze. He let out of cry of pain as she lifted his head. "This will only take a moment. We need to stop this bleeding," she said as she removed the last of the bandages. Continuing to hold his head, she wrapped fresh ones around his head. Every moment was excruciatingly painful for Reverend John, but he held his breath to steel himself. Finally, it was over and she laid his head back on the pillow.

"There now," she said as she tucked his blanket around him. "Are you comfortable?" He smiled benignly.

"Good," she said. "I'll be back to check on you later and perhaps get you some soup if you're up to it."

The thought of food nauseated him for the first time in his life.

CHAPTER THIRTY-ONE

P astor Thomas answered a knock at his office door and immediately recognized Lt. Bob McWilliams of the New Orleans Police Department. "Lt. McWilliams," he said, surprised.

"Pastor Thomas," he acknowledged as they shook hands.

"Well, come in and have a seat," the pastor said, quickly picking up some papers from a chair in front of his desk. As he took his own chair, he asked, "What can I do for you?"

"We've just arrested the alleged bomber, and I wanted to come over and tell you personally."

Pastor Thomas was momentarily stunned. "Are you sure you have the right man?"

Lt. McWilliams nodded, "Full confession. He's been a person of interest for some time, but we finally got the evidence we needed last night. When we went over to arrest him, he didn't even put up a fight. He admitted the whole thing."

Pastor Thomas sat back in his chair and looked up at the lieutenant. "Why did he do it?"

"His name is Bobby Jack Chassen. He's a member of a white supremacist group called the White Guard. Apparently there had been a lot of anger about these angel sightings, especially since…" he paused, trying to find the right words. "Well, sorry, pastor, but they hated the fact that a black church was getting publicity about them."

Pastor Thomas flinched slightly but said nothing.

"You know these extremist groups," the lieutenant continued. "They're so full of hate they can't even see straight. Well anyway, a group of them got all liquored up the night before the bombing, and they dared Bobby Jack that he didn't have the guts to do it."

Pastor Thomas stopped him. "He bombed the church and almost killed Mary Beth on a dare?"

"Yeah." His voice was cold and exact.

"Where is he now?"

"He's being booked at HQ this morning." He looked down for a moment, then back at Pastor Thomas. "Well, I just thought you'd like to know."

Pastor Thomas smiled, "I appreciate your coming over to tell me. What do you want me to do at this point?"

Lt. McWilliams stood. "The DA has already filed charges, and we'll need statements from you, but we'll be back in touch about that."

Pastor Thomas extended his hand. "Just let me know what I need to do."

CHAPTER THIRTY-TWO

"Get it, Dina," six-year-old Seda Amir said, as she held the string high in the air. "Come on, you can do it." The kitten pawed the air, just missing the string, and continued doing so until finally weary of the game she lunged, grabbing her prize, and began batting the string around the floor. Delighted, Seda kept watching until something else caught her attention. Her parents were speaking in hushed tones in another room. She moved closer to the door, where she could hear better.

"I feel it's best," Mansoor Amir said. "We must leave tonight."

"But you know what they have been saying," his wife said quickly with a look of fear in her eyes. "They will brand as infidels those who believe these Western lies and leave Iran."

Mansoor went over to his wife and placed his hands gently on her shoulders. "Nadia, even if there was not a prediction of an earthquake, I still feel we are unsafe here. I have tried many times to tell the president that the center of government should not be in Tehran, but be moved closer to Isfahan, but he would never listen. I suppose he doesn't think that a professor of geophysics knows what he's talking about."

She gave him a slight smile. "Of course you do," she said softly.

He nodded. "I do. The predictions of the other two earthquakes were correct, and they were not even in active seismic areas. We are. Do you know what a major earthquake could do to Tehran?" Nadia said nothing as she waited.

"Iran would be decimated. None of our buildings could stand even a four point earthquake. If an earthquake were to hit Tehran in what I've predicted for years to be somewhere around a seven to eight, we would lose hundreds of thousands. Even at five percent of our population, over six hundred thousand people could die."

"But what if you're wrong?" she asked in a small, frightened voice.

His eyes were gentle and contemplative. "I would rather risk losing my job than risk losing any of you."

"Papa," Seda said as she ran into the room, "Can we take Dina, too?"

Mansoor looked down at his youngest daughter with mock anger. "Seda, have you been listening at the door?"

She looked down and nodded slightly.

He knelt down to her level and lifted her chin with his finger. "Yes, Seda, you may bring Dina." She looked at him and smiled. "But you must help get her food together. Can you do that?"

"Yes, yes. Thank you," she said as she ran toward the kitchen.

"Mansoor, what about Mother?"

"Yes, tell Nasreen to come. Bita and Malak should be home any second. We will leave no later than six o'clock tonight after evening prayers. Hurry now, we have much to do."

CHAPTER THIRTY-THREE

"I'm sorry," Amanda said as she set her fork down. "I guess I'm not really hungry after all." She looked up at Mark, who was finishing the crab cakes that McCormick & Schmick's was famous for, and smiled slightly. "I guess all of this hasn't affected you as much as it has me."

"Well," he said, dabbing his mouth with his napkin, "I just show it differently." He sat back in his chair and had a sip of wine as he looked at her. "Listen, I'm sorry," he said apologetically, "I know it's been a stressful day for you."

"A dare, Mark. Pastor Thomas said Mary Beth was almost killed because of a stupid dare. What's the matter with this world? You know, I don't think it really hit me until I saw the look of concern on the pope's face. I know it hit David the same way. If the pope was worried, we should all be worried. It was just so frightening." She looked away for a moment and then back at him. "He wanted me to go back home to Portland with him, Mark. He said that Dad needs me."

Mark took a deep breath and let it out slowly. "Do you want to go?"

She shook her head slightly and looked down. "You know I can't. There's too much I have to do here."

He reached over and took her hand. "If you want to go, it's okay. God knows, we'll miss you." He hesitated a moment, then continued. "I'll miss you."

Tears clouded her eyes as she looked up at him. She smiled, unable to say anything.

"Let's get out of here," he said, signaling the waiter. As they made their way past the bar where the television was blaring the Redskins game, a CNC Breaking News Alert broke.

"Ah, come on," a man at the end of the bar shouted. Amanda and Mark stopped in their tracks.

"News sources report a massive earthquake has just hit Iran," the reporter said.

"Enough already," the man protested loudly. "Get the game back on."

"Let's get to the studio," Mark said.

Amanda looked back at Mark as they hurried out the door. "This is what she predicted, but it was supposed to hit on Sunday."

"It is Sunday in Iran right now, Amanda." He checked his watch. "Should be about six thirty."

Rain beat down on the car as they turned on the radio, but between talk shows discussing the banning of crosses in California cities, a rap station screaming raunchy lyrics and a rock and roll station belting out favorites of the sixties, there was no mention of the earthquake. Finally arriving at the studio, they found several people crowded around the monitors.

Al-Jazeera TV showed a backdrop of devastation. Buildings were crumbled and streets were littered with fallen debris. The announcer was yelling in Arabic. On another monitor, the BBC was reporting that a 7.9 earthquake struck Tehran at approximately 5:50 a.m. Hundreds of thousands of people are missing and are feared dead

"Has anyone heard from Wes?" Mark asked.

"Not since yesterday morning," Tim McPherson said. "He said he was going to try to get out early, but that he'd let us know when he was leaving. Haven't heard a thing though."

"Try to reach him," Mark said as he turned back to Amanda. "We need to get some copy together. Are you up to going on?"

She let out a breath. "Yes," she said resolutely.

"Okay, then."

Moments later, Amanda was seated at the anchor desk waiting for the director's cue.

The WNN News Alert graphic flashed on the screen and the camera zoomed to a close-up of Amanda.

"At 5:50 this morning in Iran, less than two hours ago, a 7.9 earthquake rumbled through the streets of Tehran. With over twelve million people in this city, it is feared that the injury and death toll could reach into the tens of thousands. Our own Wes Ross is standing by in Tehran."

She turned toward the monitor to see a scratchy picture of the reporter as he waited through the satellite delay. "I'm standing on the outskirts of Tehran right now, Amanda. The city is in rubble. Many buildings have been leveled. Chaos is everywhere, as survivors desperately try to dig victims out of the debris. There has already been a major aftershock which destroyed the archeological museum. Priceless artifacts dating back as far as 1500 BC have been lost, but of course, that doesn't compare to the tremendous loss of life." In the background, people could be seen running through the street.

"Moments ago," Wes continued, "I spoke with a government official who estimated that the death toll could reach eight hundred thousand or more. Makeshift morgues have already been set up throughout the city, many in unstable buildings. Obviously, clean up and rebuilding could take years."

Wes stopped as yet another aftershock began to rumble and shake the ground underneath him, knocking over a power pole directly behind him. He glanced over his shoulder at the live, crackling wires and quickly looked back toward the camera. "This is Wes Ross, reporting live from Tehran."

"Stay safe, Wes." She set her script down and focused on the camera. "This earthquake in Iran is the last one predicted by little Katie Ballard; the first one in Seoul and the second one in New York. If you've been following this story, you'll remember that Katie also said that an angel told her, 'God has loved us, but we have not loved Him.' She said the earthquakes were a sign from God."

"I'll be honest," Amanda said, continuing, "I am as baffled about these angel sightings as you may be. Two months ago I probably would have said that this may have been a plot by some extremist group, for what purpose I have no idea, but as I have come to know the people who claim they have seen the angels, I can tell you that most of these people are absolutely sincere. I believe they are telling the truth. I realize that these days, it isn't politically correct to mention God. We've shoved religion into the back closet, because it's no longer fashionable—almost an embarrassment. I can tell you though, if God exists, and I believe He does, with the state that the world is in today, He can't be pleased with us. In my career as a reporter, I have covered wars, murders, crimes against children, corrupt politicians and business people, and so many other stories that show what has happened to mankind. Our values and our morals have reached such a low point that we've become insensitive to the garbage that is thrown at us from television and movies, sensationalizing the atrocities of the world."

Amanda paused a moment before continuing. "Ladies and gentlemen, whatever your beliefs, I feel that these angel sightings are a wake-up call to all of us. Our prayers tonight go with the earthquake victims in Seoul, in New York, and in Tehran. This is Amanda Fox. Good evening." The red camera light went out and Amanda slumped back in her chair.

Mark came over and gave her an enigmatic smile. "Went a bit off script, huh?"

She raised both hands and shook her head. "Don't say it. It's just... I couldn't help it. We both saw the angel on the tape. I know now that all of this is real. It is a wake-up call, Mark, and I just had to tell them."

"Well," he said softly, "I'm proud of you. It took courage to do that. You realize, though, you've just made yourself an open target, don't you?"

She gave him a hint of a smile. "It's not the first time."

CHAPTER THIRTY-FOUR

R ain pounded against Amanda's bedroom window, finally stirring her from a fitful sleep and a long night. She managed to fall asleep at 1:30, but then woke up at 3:30 and again at 4:45 and finally at 5:38. She glanced at the clock which said 9:35. Good heavens, she thought, I haven't slept this late in years. She threw off the covers, went into the bathroom, and washed her face. As she glanced up at the mirror, she saw dark circles under her eyes. Glad I don't have to go on air today, she thought.

Wrapping herself quickly in her robe, she went to retrieve the three newspapers outside her door. Throughout the week she had received her news from the computer, the wire services, and the station, but Sundays were different. She enjoyed leisurely reading the papers with a cup or two of coffee. Her freezer held her prized stock of Kona beans that she brought back from her last Hawaii trip.

As she whirled the beans in the grinder, the rich coffee scent filled the kitchen. Waiting for the coffee to brew, she unfolded each of the papers on the counter and scanned the headlines. She read in The New York Times, "Massive Earthquake hits Tehran," and the story continued with descriptions of how geologists predicted this quake several years ago. Several articles compared it with New York's recent earthquake, but no mention was made of Katie's prediction.

Flipping through the pages, her eye caught an extremely worried caricature of herself in a political cartoon. An old man with long robes holding a sign that said, "Repent, the end is near" was standing on a soapbox. Amanda was beside him with a Trinity Broadcast Network microphone asking, "Can you define 'near'?"

She threw it aside, poured herself a cup of coffee, and picked up the Washington Times, whose headlines also covered the earthquake. Their article, though, focused more on the political repercussions in the capital city of Iran. Several top members of the Islamic Coalition Society, Iran's most liberal and radical voice, had been killed. The president of Iran was in critical condition and his more conservative vice president had taken control of the country.

The last paper, the Los Angeles Times, featured a similar headline detailing the earthquake, with several smaller articles discussing the possibility of the "big one" in LA. As she flipped through the paper, she stopped when she saw an article discussing the "alleged" angel sightings. It asked more questions than it answered and went on to say that CNC's Matt Engle was going to "expose the true stories of the sightings on his Sunday morning show, The Real Story with Matt Engle at 10:00 a.m. EST." Amanda quickly checked her watch. It was now 9:50. She grabbed her phone and punched in Mark's number.

"Hi, it's me. CNC's going to do a show on the angel sightings this morning at ten."

"That should be an interesting slant," he said. "You doing okay?"

"It was a miserable night," she said with a yawn. "I kept waking up. The last time I looked at the clock it was five thirty and the next thing I knew it was nine thirty, I'm embarrassed to say."

"Stress will do that to you. Get yourself some coffee, and I'll call you after the show."

She turned on the living room television to CNC. Paula Walters was interviewing Cher. Amanda hit the mute button and went back to the kitchen to pour another cup of coffee. When she returned, the program had ended, and a commercial was playing. When Matt Engle finally came on, she un-muted the television. The dark-haired young reporter sat on a barstool, studying the script in his hand as he waited for the solo flugelhorn intro music to subside. He looked into the camera when the last note was played. "Good morning. I'm Matt Engle. Welcome to the Real Story."

Matt paused a moment for effect. "Angels. Are they real? According to recent news reports, some people think so. Within the last several weeks, reports have surfaced from people all over the world who not only claim to have seen angels but have had conversations with them as well. Almost as if scripted, they each have recited the same ominous words, 'Prepare yourselves; the time is at hand.' We at the Real Story wanted to know the truth behind these alleged sightings. Who are these people who have claimed to see angels? Why are they doing this? Our investigation has revealed some surprising answers."

For the next half hour, Matt detailed each of the people who have seen the angels, beginning with Ellie LeBeaux. Through taped conversations with others, Ellie LeBeaux was portrayed as a demented old lady who brought cookies to the cemetery. They even found one old man who claimed she was hysterically out of control at one point and had to be sedated and taken to the hospital. He described her as "extremely unstable."

The scene switched to Peru, where Manuel Guzman, who was currently in prison for robbery, was described by people as a violent person who was generally known to be a thief and a liar. They interviewed a market owner who said that Guzman had stolen numerous times from his store, and that he was in prison where he belonged.

In Victoria, British Columbia, Matt interviewed several people about little Katie Ballard. He said he spoke to a woman who described Katie as an impressionable young girl. He showed the church that the Ballard family "faithfully attend," leaving the impression that her family carried their religion to an extreme and little Katie couldn't help but be caught in it. He also interviewed someone who said that Katie had a gift for seeing the future, and therefore it was not a surprise to him that she could predict the earthquakes. As for the rest of the people who claimed to see angels, Matt dismissed them as copy cats.

The next segment focused on Reverend John Winters. Matt showed a sound bite of Reverend John with tears in his eyes, telling how an angel appeared before him and told him to raise money for a great temple. The scene then switched to Baton Rouge, where Matt was standing in front of the Spirit of Truth Church. Detailing Reverend John's background, Matt told his viewers how he has duped his followers—giving specific details, including speaking tours, the phony charities, the Swiss bank accounts, the palatial mansions throughout the world, the yachts, the jets, and how convicted con artist Benny McDuff was his bag man. He ended the segment with news that Benny McDuff had died in the New York earthquake and that Reverend John has presumably gone into hiding.

Matt ended the program with his opinion that these people who had claimed to see angels were in some way connected to the Spirit of Truth Church for the sole purpose of frightening people into a religious fervor—and thereby enriching the church. Unfortunately, he added, some members of the press were also duped and played into their hands. Amanda, seething with rage, punched off the television and grabbed her phone. Mark was faster and Amanda answered on the first ring.

"Would you believe that?" Amanda's fury almost choked her. "He's made us all sound like addle-brained idiots. Unbelievable! And poor Miss Ellie; he made her look stupid and senile, and Katie and her family like religious zealots. How could he say such things? CNC's going to be sued big time over Matt's little show."

"Calm down a minute, Amanda. Lawsuits will come later. Scolesco's not going to let this one go by, but think for a minute what he said about Reverend John. Wasn't that your information you got from April?"

"So?" Amanda said, still breathing hard.

"Well, you have to say, he's been doing his homework. Interesting info about Benny McDuff, though—I hadn't heard that he died."

Amanda stopped. "No, I haven't either. Do you think Reverend John's really in hiding? Maybe he was caught in the earthquake, too."

"Who knows? He might be dead as well."

"Probably not. If they found Benny, Reverend John wouldn't be too far from him. My bet is that he's either lying somewhere injured or has somehow managed to get away. Either way, he's not our biggest problem. We need to work on damage control right now. You need to come out firing on your show tomorrow about the attack that Matt has lodged on you, Ellie, and on Katie's family. You owe this to them. If she'd do it, we need to interview Ellie again, to show the viewers that this remarkable, intelligent woman bears no resemblance to the demented old lady Matt portrayed. I think we should also interview Katie's parents and have them discuss their views on Katie's experience and have them talk about their church. The Ballards are great people and the world needs to see this."

"I know," she said in a normal tone of voice, finally calming down herself. "There's a lot to do. I'll be in the studio in an hour."

"Atta girl. See you there."

CHAPTER THIRTY-FIVE

Atta girl, Amanda thought to herself. She took a deep breath and let it out slowly as she watched raindrops run down the window. And so begins another day, she thought.

When Amanda arrived at the studio, Mark was already there speaking with April. He saw her approaching and gave her a wave.

"It's Sunday, April. What are you doing here?" she asked surprised.

"Mark called me in. We've just been talking about the bloodletting on CNC this morning. They're just readying the tape for me."

"You didn't see the show?" Amanda asked.

"No, I haven't seen CNC in years. It's my little policy of keeping purity in the home."

"Good policy," Amanda said with a laugh. "I'm going to grab some tea."

She hung her raincoat on the rack in her office and made her way to the coffee room. As her tea was steeping, April ran in, slightly out of breath.

"Amanda, remember that guy you kept trying to reach in Greece?"

"Niko? Yeah, why?"

"He's on the phone for you right now."

Without another word, Amanda raced back to her office and

punched in the line. "This is Amanda Fox," she said as professionally as she could without sounding out of breath.

"Ms. Fox, this Niko Gravari. You remember who I am? My sister, she met you in Roma."

"Yes, Mr. Gravari, I do remember you. I'm happy to speak to you at last."

Niko hesitated a moment, then said. "Tonight I watched television. I saw the man say the people who say they saw angels were crazy, and they were lying. I saw the angel, Ms. Fox. I'm not crazy. I saw her and I am telling the truth. I…I just wanted to tell you."

"Thank you for calling me, Mr. Gravari, and I want you to know that I believe you. I saw the program on CNC myself and I can tell you that this man was not telling the truth. I know what the truth is and I know that these angel sightings are real. Niko, I saw an angel, too."

"You did?" he asked quickly.

"Yes, she was on the tape when we interviewed a little girl from Canada. I only saw her for a moment, and then she was gone."

"You tell viewers this?"

Amanda was silent for a moment. "I haven't yet, but I will on my show tomorrow." She thought for a moment. "Niko, if I can get a camera crew to Kalymnos would you be willing to do an interview with me?"

"No, no. I don't know about that."

"Niko, I know it's been difficult for you, but it's important for people to see you and to know that you are telling the truth. I know that you are. The rest of the world needs to know that, too."

After a moment he asked quietly, "What do I have to do?"

"I'll ask you questions about what happened and just tell me the truth, Niko. That's all I want."

"Okay, I will."

"I need to make some phone calls. Where can I reach you?"

Niko gave her the phone number, and she told him she would be back in touch. When she hung up, she checked her watch. It was now 1:07 p.m. It would be 8:07 p.m. right now in Kalymnos.

She raced out of her office. "Mark, that was Niko Gravari from

Greece. He's agreed to an interview on the show tomorrow. Do we have anyone over there that could go to Kalymnos?"

"I think Bob Keegan is in Rome right now. I'll make some calls. In the meantime, April, you need to get to the editing room to see that CNC tape. Make notes of each accusation that Matt throws out, so that we can counter each one. And Amanda, as soon as you can, line up Ellie and the Ballards. Let me know."

Amanda went back to her office and immediately called Bethany Baptist Church. The morning service had let out ten minutes ago, and she hoped someone would be in the office. The phone answered on the third ring. "This is Bethany Baptist Church," a young lady's voice said.

"Hello, this is Amanda Fox. Would Pastor Thomas be in his office by any chance?"

"No, he's still at the church."

"Would you give him a message for me?"

"Okay, just a minute," she said as she searched for a paper and pen. "Okay, I'm ready."

"This is Amanda Fox," Amanda repeated. "And if Pastor Thomas could call me right away, I would appreciate it." Amanda gave her the phone number three times before the girl could get it right. "Please tell him it's very important."

"Okay."

She then called Ellie, but the phone rang several times without an answer. She must still be at the church, Amanda thought.

Knowing that the Ballards would also be in church at the moment, she thought she might at least leave a message.

A man answered, "Hello."

"Mr. Ballard?"

"Yes, who is this?"

"Amanda Fox with WNN News. I was the one who did the interview with Katie. I'm happy to reach you. I thought you might be at church."

"Why?" Charley said coldly. "Because we're such religious zealots?"

"Oh, you must have seen the CNC program this morning."

"Don't you mean a pack-of-lies? Caroline is very upset about it."

"I'm sure she must be. I was, too. I still am. This was journalism at its worst. Mr. Ballard, I'm so sorry this has hurt your family. I know beyond a shadow of a doubt that Katie was telling the truth. I know that she saw an angel."

"Why is it that you think you know so much?"

"Because I saw the angel, too. When we brought the tape back to the studio, our editor, the cameraman, the producer, and I saw her sitting between Katie and me. She was looking up at Katie and holding her hand. When we went to show it that night, though, the angel had disappeared."

Charley was silent.

Amanda continued, "I'm as angry about Matt Engle's show as I know you are, so I'm doing a show tomorrow to counter all of his allegations. I intend to tell the viewers about seeing the angel myself. A man from Greece, who has been called crazy because he said he's seen an angel, has agreed to come on as well. He wants people to know the truth. I would like you as a family to be interviewed as well. Matt Engle made all of us look foolish, and I'm not going to let him get away with it. The only way to counter him is to show the world what wonderful people you are. Would you be willing to come on the show?"

"I don't know," he said softly. "I'll discuss it with Caroline and let you know."

"Of course. Caroline has my number." Amanda hung up and stared at the phone for a moment, lost in thought. Matt Engle may have caused the problem, but ultimately she was responsible for putting people in this position. Last night's performance and tomorrow night's show may very well be the end of her career, but there was no turning back now. She didn't know if there was any way to make things whole again for these people, but she was going to try. The ring of her phone startled her and she immediately picked it up.

"Amanda Fox."

"Ms. Fox, it's Pastor Thomas."

"Oh, thank you for calling me back. I know Sundays are terribly busy for you, but I wanted to let you know about a program that was aired on CNC today."

"Yes, I know about it."

"Did you see it?"

"No, I was with the Sunday school this morning, but several people came up to me after church today and told me about it. They said it did not cast a good light on our Miss Ellie."

"That's true," Amanda said quietly, "Miss Ellie did not deserve that. The reporter was way out of bounds with his lies, especially when he said Miss Ellie was hysterical and had to be sedated. I don't know how he thinks he can get away with that, but I promise you, he won't."

"Ms. Fox, he didn't lie. I was with Miss Ellie when it happened. It was many years ago, shortly after her husband had died. She had come for a meeting at the church and I was walking with her outside when her daughter came and told her that her son had been killed in combat. It was more than she could take, and she fell to the ground, weeping inconsolably. She wouldn't let us take her home or even into the church. She needed help, so we called the paramedics who sedated her and took her to the hospital."

"Poor Miss Ellie," Amanda said sadly, "to have to go through all she has and now to have some young, stupid reporter skew the truth and try to make a name for himself at her expense. It's still unbeliev-able. Was she at church this morning?"

"Of course."

"How was she?"

"She was as fine and dignified and strong as she always is."

"Pastor Thomas, I'm doing a show tomorrow night on the angel sightings. I don't know how you feel about it, but I'm going to ask Miss Ellie if she'll consider doing an interview with me."

"I'm not sure that's the best idea right now."

"I think it's the only option we have for Miss Ellie's sake. I want the world to know what kind of a person she really is, and not the disparaging picture Matt Engle painted of her. The entire program was so very unfair to everyone—including Katie Ballard and her family—

and I want to set the record straight." She was quiet for a moment and then continued, "I owe it to these people."

"Ms. Fox, you're not responsible for Matt Engle's program."

"No, but because I've interviewed them, they've all become targets and unfairly so. I suppose the only good that came out of his show was the segment on Reverend John."

"What about him?"

"Matt exposed all the illegal activities he's been involved in—including all the false charities he had set up. He even talked about how his money was filtered through Swiss bank accounts and how he used the money to provide yachts, jets, and palatial mansions for himself."

"Thanks be to God," Pastor Thomas said quietly.

"Yes," she agreed. "He, at least, has been stopped. Apparently, he's in hiding right now, but when he surfaces, I think he'll be spending a lot of time behind bars. Matt Engle linked all the people who had seen angels with the Spirit of Truth Church and implied they were all working together. That's another reason for doing the show tomorrow. These lies have got to be stopped."

"I don't know if Miss Ellie would even consider doing another interview, but if she doesn't, I want you to know that I think you are right. The lies must be stopped. Would you like me to speak to her for you?"

"Yes, I would, thank you. I tried calling her at home earlier, but there was no answer. If you could let me know as soon as you know, I'd appreciate it. I'll be in the studio all day today," she paused before continuing. "Thank you again."

"You're very welcome. I'll see what I can do."

She sat back in her chair, thinking of her next move. Calls were made, wheels were set in motion, and now all she could do was wait. She looked up to see Mark coming toward her office.

"Bob took the first plane to Athens. Should be there in a couple of hours. He said he'd call as soon as he arrives."

Amanda checked her watch. It was still only 8:35 p.m. in Athens. "Good, let me call Niko and tell him that our cameraman will contact him in the morning," she said as she punched in the numbers. As she spoke to Niko, Mark took a seat in her office and waited.

"Well, that's at least one," she said as she hung up. "I'm still waiting for the Ballards' call. Mr. Ballard was understandably unhappy, but he said he'd talk to Caroline. I hope they decide to come on the show."

"How about Ellie?"

"I couldn't reach her, so I called the church. Pastor Thomas said he'd talk to Ellie for me, and I told him how much I'd appreciate it. I don't know, though. I really should be talking to her myself."

"I'd leave it alone. If you really want her to come on the show, it's nice to get a little help."

"It's just that the waiting to nail it down is hard."

"I know. In the meantime, I called the New York Times and got confirmation on Benny McDuff's death. I asked specifically about Reverend John and they said they had no information."

"So he could be lying by the pool somewhere in the Bahamas."

"Could be."

CHAPTER THIRTY-SIX

At the Convent of the Sacred Heart a doctor stood by Reverend John's bed, checking his chart. He looked down at John over the top of his glasses. "How's the head?"

"Better," Reverend John lied, despite the fact that his head was still throbbing. He knew that the more he complained, the longer he would be kept at the convent, and he wanted desperately to go home.

The doctor nodded and made a note on his chart. "I think you should be able to travel tomorrow. Your vital signs are all good and the head injury is healing nicely. You'll still experience headaches from time to time, but that's to be expected. I'll send film with you for your doctor along with prescriptions that you can fill as soon as you return."

Joy raced through Reverend John's heart. He was finally going home. He shifted his legs under the covers and felt the weight of his cast. "How much longer do I have to wear this cast?"

"At least another six weeks. You had a bad break, but it is healing well, and you should be fine. You'll still have to take it easy for the next few weeks, but I'm sure you'll be more comfortable at home. Is there someone we can call for you?"

Reverend John's first thought was of Benny. How was he going to get along without him? He needed to think through the situation and figure out his next moves. It wasn't going to be easy by himself. He just needed to get home—maybe back to Florida.

"Yes," he said. "I need you to call my pilot, Dave Price. He'll arrange transportation for me." He gave the doctor Dave's phone number, then asked if he could have an ambulance take him to the airport.

"I'm afraid getting an ambulance right now is going to be difficult, but you'll be fine in a taxi. I'll have one here for you tomorrow morning around nine."

"Thank you, doctor," he said. He didn't care if he had to crawl to the airport. He just wanted to leave this place and go home.

CHAPTER THIRTY-SEVEN

Unceasing rain continued to pound the city Monday morning as the taxi pulled into the driveway of the Convent of the Sacred Heart. For the last fifty-five minutes, Reverend John had waited impatiently by the window for it to arrive. When at last he saw the beat-up old Checker Cab, he called out to Sister Mary Margaret, "He's here."

"Now don't move too fast," she said as she took his arm. "Sister," she said to another nun close by, "could you give me a hand? I need to help him out to the car. Bring these crutches and be careful now, it's going to be slippery out there." The other nun took the crutches with one hand and helped support Reverend John with the other. Between the two of them, they managed to slowly walk him to the waiting taxi.

"Take care of yourself now," Sister Mary Margaret said, putting the crutches in the back seat beside Reverend John and tucking a blanket around him. "Don't overdo it," she said. She closed the door and gave him a quick wave through the rain-streaked window. The two nuns hurried back into the convent.

"You were supposed to be here at nine," Reverend John said coldly to the driver.

"Listen, man," the driver said as he looked into the mirror. "Everything's flooded. I had to go ten miles out of my way just to get here. So, where to?"

"Teterboro airport."

"Well, I just heard that the Lincoln Tunnel is closed, so they're diverting all the traffic to the G.W. Bridge. I'll get you there, but it's going to be slow," he said as he pulled away from the curb.

At Teterboro, three gentlemen sat in a quiet corner of the ornate corporate jet boarding lounge, patiently waiting as they casually read newspapers and magazines. Rain had cancelled or delayed most of the day's flights, so the waiting area was mostly empty except for two corporate pilots and another gentleman, dressed in a brown raincoat, who was talking loudly into his cell phone ear-piece—much to the annoyance of everyone.

Dave checked his watch and glanced out the window at the rain. "I'm going to get an update on the weather," he said to the other pilot as he got up to leave.

"Okay," Ken said. "I'll stay here and wait for him."

"No, no," shouted the man into the cell phone. "We've got to stay with the game plan. We can get that property at our price if we just wait them out." He paused. "Yeah, yeah, I know, but you can't panic yet. Listen, this guy's late and I'm not going to sit around here and wait for him. I'm grabbing a cab to LaGuardia. If I have to fly commercial, I'll fly commercial. I'll see you tomorrow." He clicked off his phone, grabbed his briefcase, and headed for the door.

The room was instantly quiet. The only sound that could be heard was the pelting rain hitting the large windows. Out on the ramp, Reverend John's Gulfstream IV was visible through the glass. Dave came back and noticed the guy on the cell phone was gone.

He smiled, "Lost Chatty Cathy, huh?"

"Yeah. So, what's up?"

"Well, if we can get out of here within the hour, we should be okay," he said as he glanced at his watch. "After that, we may have to wait until tomorrow because another huge band of weather is coming in right after this. Problem is, it's raining everywhere—even in Florida."

"I've never seen it so bad."

"I'm going to go start the APU," Dave said as he zipped his jacket. "This plane needs to be warmed up. At least that will give us a head start. Stay here and wait for him. From what they said, he's going to need some help getting out to the plane." He went to the door, punched in the exit code, and jogged out through the rain.

Minutes later, Reverend John finally came through the door, slowly hobbling on crutches. Ken went over to help him.

"Oh, Ken, where's Dave?"

"He's warming up the plane. Let me help you," he said as he took a crutch and put his arm under him. "Lean on me. It will be easier."

As they went step by step toward the door, the three gentlemen stood up and approached them. "Are you Reverend John Winters?" one of the gentlemen asked.

They both stopped. "Yes," Reverend John replied. "Who are you?" The man reached inside of his pocket and flashed a badge. "FBI." Fear coursed through Reverend John's body as he stared at the men. "Wha…what do you want?" he stammered.

"John Winters, you are under arrest for tax evasion and fraud," he said as he produced a pair of handcuffs from his pocket and clicked half on Reverend John's right wrist. "You have the right to remain silent," he continued as he pulled Reverend John's arm behind him, shoving the pilot out of the way, and clicked the other half on his left wrist. Without support, Reverend John momentarily lost his balance and the other FBI agent came around to steady him. "Anything you say, can and will be held against you," the first agent continued.

They were interrupted by Dave Price storming through the door. "What's going on?" he demanded. "There are people locking down the plane."

The FBI agent ignored him and continued with the Miranda rights until he was finished.

"We're taking John Winters in," he said to the pilot. "The Gulfstream is now impounded. You two are free to go after you give us names, addresses, and phone numbers in case we need to reach you."

Reverend John looked out at his beautiful Gulfstream IV, the entry door now covered with gaudy orange stickers, and watched through the rain-streaked glass as the wheels were being chained to the tarmac. He looked at Dave Price as his own eyes pooled with tears. "I'm sorry," he said as he shook his head. "I'm just so sorry," he whispered as the FBI agents slowly escorted him out the door.

CHAPTER THIRTY-EIGHT

A manda studied the notes on the Matt Engle tape that April had given her and made notes to herself as she prepared the script for her evening program. Unbelievable, she thought to herself, as she read Matt's outrageous allegations against Miss Ellie and the Ballards. She was focusing so intently that she jumped when she heard Mark's voice.

"Did you hear me?" he asked.

She looked up, startled. "No, sorry, what?"

"Bob Keegan just called. He's in Kalymnos and has contacted Niko Gravari. He told him they were going to shoot it live tonight at 9:30— 4:30 a.m. Kalymnos time. He said Niko didn't have a problem with the time since he's usually up early for sponge diving. I think it's going to be more of a problem for Bob, but he said they'd be ready."

"Good," Amanda said as she leaned back and held her pen between her hands. "I had a phone call from Caroline Ballard this morning. She said they would be willing to go on air as well. I've already contacted KCPQ in Seattle and they're sending a cameraman and reporter. They'll be there around 5:30 this evening, so we'll be ready to tape around 6:00 their time."

"Which reporter is going?" Mark asked since he knew most of the reporters in Seattle, having moved from there.

"Dennis Edwards. Do you know him?"

"Yeah, I do. We worked together at KOMO. He's a good man."

"Still haven't heard from Pastor Thomas or Miss Ellie, though. I'll give them another half hour and then I'll call."

"Sorry to interrupt you," April said as she handed Mark a piece of paper. "This just came across from AP."

Mark took a second to scan the article. "Well, that answers that," he said, as he handed the paper to Amanda.

She read the story and quickly looked up at Mark. "They got him?"

"Yeah," Mark said. "I guess the feds move fast when there's evidence of tax evasion. So, until the trial he's under house arrest at his Baton Rouge home."

"They should have just locked him up," said April with a trace of bitterness. "I mean, geez, you can't feel too sorry for him at home."

"These days you can plea bargain for anything," Amanda said. "But the important thing is that he's no longer able to dupe people." Amanda's cell phone rang, and she quickly answered it.

"Ms. Fox?"

Amanda immediately recognized Ellie's voice and motioned for Mark to wait a moment. "Yes, Miss Ellie, how are you?"

"I'm fine, thank you," Ellie responded with the same measured cadence as always. "I'm here in Pastor Thomas' office with my daughter right now. Pastor Thomas has told me about your program tonight and that you would like to interview me."

"Yes," Amanda said. "The CNC program unfairly depicted you and the others who have seen the angels. I just want people to know who you really are, and that Matt Engle's story was completely false."

"All right, Ms. Fox, I will be on your program tonight. May I ask you a favor, though?"

"Certainly."

"Would it be possible to have my daughter and Pastor Thomas with me? I would feel much more comfortable."

"Of course. Thank you, Miss Ellie. If I could speak to Pastor Thomas for a moment, I'll let him know about the arrangements."

After they spoke, she hung up and looked at Mark and April, still waiting by the door. "It's a go."

"And five," the director said as he silently held up his fingers for the countdown starting Amanda's show.

"Good evening. As many of you know, there have been numerous reports of people who claim that they have actually seen angels. Not only have sightings happened all over the world, but each of these people have said the same thing—that God has sent the angels to bring a message to the world. A recent news program has stated that the people making these claims are simply lying to further some sort of hidden agenda. Tonight, I want you to meet some of these people and to hear their stories and make the determination yourself. Joining us from Kalymnos, Greece, is Niko Gravari, who will tell about his experience for the first time tonight; from New Orleans, Ellie LeBeaux; and from British Columbia, Katie Ballard and her family."

"You're doing great," Mark said from the control booth. Amanda listened through her earpiece as he continued, "Bob said Niko is extremely nervous. Go to Ellie first, then the Ballards, and save Niko for last."

"Let's go first to New Orleans where Ellie LeBeaux is joined by her daughter, Georgia Fontaine and Pastor James Thomas, the minister of Bethany Baptist Church. Welcome all." They smiled and nodded in acknowledgment.

"Ellie, can you tell us about your experience?"

As Ellie recounted her story about the angel in the cemetery, Amanda listened quietly. "And you've told me you had a second sighting?"

"Yes," she said. "It was in my home. This time it was a little boy."

She proceeded to tell the story of how she found him sitting at her kitchen table. "He told me that God had another message. He said that the children of God have defied His laws. They have hurt the smallest among them. They have lost reverence for Him and for their brothers and sisters and he said that God wanted me to tell the people to prepare themselves, for the time is at hand. Then the boy looked at me and said, 'Be strong.' He touched my cheek, and then he vanished."

"Miss Ellie," Amanda asked. "Why do you think you were chosen?"

"I don't know." She replied quietly. "But I feel very blessed."

"Georgia, you must be very proud of your mother."

"I've always been. She's been a wonderful mother to all of us children, and she's the most giving person I know." Ellie smiled at her and squeezed her hand.

"Pastor Thomas, how long have you known Ellie?"

"I've been fortunate to know her twenty-three years now, since I first became the minister of Bethany Baptist Church."

"How long has Ellie been a member of the church?"

"Much longer than I have—over seventy-four years."

"And in all that time, have you ever known her to stretch the truth?"

"Never," he said.

"The news program I mentioned earlier has accused Ellie of losing control. Have you ever seen her lose control?"

"Only once," he said quietly as he reached over and put his hand on Ellie's. "Her husband had passed away and she was understandably sad. Not two weeks later she was told that her son had been killed in Vietnam. She was so overcome with tears and grief that paramedics had no choice but to sedate her and take her to the hospital. It was a very difficult time."

"I know it must have been. I'm angered that some reporters do not take the time to check their facts before they hurl accusations at innocent people," she said, shaking her head. "Pastor Thomas," she continued, "do you believe that angels have actually visited Ellie?"

"I have no doubt."

"Thank you all for being with us tonight." She looked back at the camera. "We'll be right back with Katie Ballard from British Columbia."

The red camera light went out and Mark said, "Great comment

about reporters not checking facts before they make allegations. You're making Matt Engle look ridiculous."

"Good," she said with a grin. "There's more to come."

"And five," the director said as the camera light came back on.

"We're talking about angel sightings tonight and the people who claim to have seen them. Joining us from British Columbia is Katie Ballard and her parents, Charley and Caroline Ballard. Thank you so much for being with us tonight." Caroline and Katie smiled while Charley sat resolutely, without expression.

"Not long ago, I spoke with Katie. We have a clip from that interview that I want to show you." As they ran the interview, the fuzziness where the angel appeared was still on the tape.

"As you all know, the earthquakes Katie predicted have all happened. Mrs. Ballard, tell me about Katie. Has she always been this intuitive?"

Caroline shook her head slightly. "No, nothing like this has ever happened before."

"Tell us about your Katie. How would you describe her?"

Caroline Ballard looked at her daughter and gave her a smile. "Katie is many things. She's loving and caring. It hasn't been easy on her to go to the hospital for her dialysis treatments, but she never complains. Her patience is amazing, as well as her inner strength just to do some of the things she's had to do."

"Mr. Ballard, could you add anything to that?"

Charley Ballard looked directly into the camera. "Yes, she's honest," he said firmly. "We've taught our girls to do the right things and to always tell the truth and that the measure of a person is their word."

"More people need to learn that lesson," Amanda said. "Katie, have you decided what you'd like to be when you grow up?"

"Um, a nurse."

"Why?"

"I don't know. They're so nice to me at the hospital that I want to do something nice for other kids and then maybe they won't feel so scared."

"Katie, were you scared when you saw the angel at the hospital?"

"Oh, no."

"Why not?"

"Because she told me not to be. She said God loves me."

"Can you tell me again what she looked like?"

"She was a little girl angel with wings and she was so pretty. She had blond hair, and it was curly like mine."

Amanda nodded in acknowledgment, remembering that was exactly the angel that she, Mark, Pete, and Joe had seen on the tape. "Katie, some people don't believe you saw an angel, but I do. Do you know why?"

"Why?"

"Because I saw her, too. After we spoke to you, we came back to our studio and ran the tape. Four of us saw her sitting between you and me. She was looking at you and holding your hand."

"Really?" asked Katie.

"Really. When we ran the tape for the television audience, she was reduced to a blur and you can still see the blur on the tape now. I will never forget her, though. You know what I think?"

"What?"

"I think she's there with you all the time, holding your hand and keeping you safe."

Katie leaned back and smiled at her mother.

"Thank you for being with us tonight. We'll be right back." The camera light went out. Amanda leaned forward and clasped her hands. "I wonder what Scolesco will think of that?"

"Yeah, me too," she heard Mark say.

Off in the shadows, by the back wall of the control booth, Martin Scolesco watched with his arms crossed.

"And five," the director once again said.

"We're talking with people who claim that they have seen angels. Joining us from Kalymnos, Greece, is Niko Gravari. Thank you, Mr. Gravari, for being with us tonight, especially since it's seven hours later and quite early in the morning there."

Niko nodded his head and said nothing.

"Niko, tell me what happened the night you saw an angel?"

"It was late. I had been diving for sponges and was walking home along beach. A lady called me. I didn't know her. She called again. 'Who are you?' I said to her. She said God chose me to give message to world."

"What was the message?" Amanda asked.

"She said to tell people that God has loved them, but they have not loved Him. She said to tell people to prepare, that God is coming."

"What happened then?"

"I don't know. I thought she was some crazy woman. But then she said not to be afraid, that God loves me. And then… she touched my cheek with her finger, and then she just…she just desparu…disappeared."

"How long ago did this happen?"

"Three months now."

"Did you tell anyone?"

"Yeah," he grunted. "But they think I'm crazy."

"Why do you want to tell people now?"

"Because I saw her. She's real. I want people to know. These other people who said they saw angels are telling the truth. They're real."

"They are real, Niko. God is sending us a very important message. Thank you for coming to the show tonight." Amanda turned toward the camera. "Ladies and gentlemen, I have to be honest with you. As an investigative reporter, I constantly fight the 'spin.' It has always been more important for me to be skeptical and to question so that I can uncover and report the truth. During the course of my investigations on these sightings, though, my skepticism has given way to profound belief and was finally confirmed with my own sighting. Whether you believe or not is your decision. I report the truth as I see it. This is Amanda Fox. Good evening."

The red light went out and Mark felt a hand on his shoulder. He turned to see Martin Scolesco. "Interesting program," he said. "I think maybe it's time for me to go back to my office and pray that the sponsors don't all pull out. Maybe the angels will put in a good word."

CHAPTER THIRTY-NINE

They gathered in a large conference room at the Aerospace Corporation's headquarters in El Segundo, California, on Tuesday morning. There were about 50 people, including astronomers and scientists from NASA, MIT, the Russian Federal Nuclear Center, the Polish Space Office, the Lawrence Livermore National Laboratory, and experts from several universities throughout the world. They were quietly speaking in groups as they waited for President Brent Hewell to arrive.

"From what I've gathered from our sources at Mauna Kea," Bob McKinnon from MIT said, "this comet is approaching Earth much faster than anyone expected."

"But there's still time to deflect it, isn't there?" Marsh Brown from Stanford asked. "I mean, it's still difficult to see it with the naked eye."

"I actually saw it last night for the first time," McKinnon replied. "If I hadn't been with Dr. Abramson, I might have mistaken it for a bright star, but he said it is definitely Comet Wilson. Still, I'm certain there's time to alter its course. Look around you at the people gathered in this room right now. These are the most brilliant minds on earth. They were already formulating solutions to this problem before this meeting even began."

The door opened at the back of the room and the president of Aerospace Corporation, Dr. Michael Patrick, led two gentlemen in black suits into the room. President Hewell and U.S. Space Force General Charles Richards immediately followed. The men in the suits took their positions beside the double doors as the president and the general took their seats along the front row of the conference room. Dr. Patrick continued to the podium and switched on the microphone.

"Please, take your seats. Time is short today and we have much to cover." After all the attendees were seated and the room was quiet, Dr. Patrick continued. "Mr. President, General Richards, distinguished fellow scientists, I want to thank you all for being here today. Not since the cataclysm that destroyed the dinosaurs has the world faced the unprecedented danger that we face today. Comet Wilson is a comet of astronomical size. Our nearest calculations indicate that the nucleus alone is approximately 250 kilometers, roughly 155 miles wide. Compare this to Hale-Bopp, with one of the largest nucleus ever recorded, and it was only forty kilometers wide." He pressed a button and a projection screen lowered to the right of him. With another click, a full-color photo of Jupiter flashed on the screen.

"In 1993, Comet Shoemaker-Levy 9 was on a rotational path toward Jupiter." He clicked another photo showing a clear picture of the comet with Jupiter in the distance. "This was taken from Mauna-Kea in March 1994." The comet could be seen in a blur streaking across the night sky. Another click and the photo revealed the break-up of the comet. "As Shoemaker-Levy 9 entered Jupiter's immense gravitational field, the comet broke up into twenty-one fragments, with the largest one, designated Fragment G, measuring just over two kilometers."

Another click and a very clear photo of Jupiter could be seen, this time with several pock marks on the planet's surface. "This is a photo from the Hubble Telescope. Although all the fragments of Comet Shoemaker-Levy 9 hit the surface in a fiery twenty-one-gun salute, Fragments G and K made the largest impacts. Fragment G created the largest crater you see there. The width of that crater is the size of Earth. The explosion of G alone was equivalent to six million tons of TNT."

Another click and the screen went blank. His face was grim as he continued. "Comet Wilson is on a direct path to Earth. If it is not altered and it passes through the gravity window, our keyhole in space, there is no question that our planet faces total destruction. Our focus today is to change its path."

A scientist from MIT spoke up. "When is the impact predicted?"

"I'll turn that question over to Dr. Steven Hoshiwara," he said as he stood to one side and waited for Dr. Hoshiwara to come to the podium.

Dr. Hoshiwara adjusted the microphone before answering the question. "We've been monitoring Comet Wilson over the last two weeks. Originally, the speed was approximately forty miles per second and was calculated at that time to be on an elliptical path around Earth—with its closest point being three hundred thousand miles away. However, this comet is unlike any we have ever tracked before.

"The speed is now calculated at an unprecedented eighty miles per second, and it appears to be speeding up. Whether this is due to its massive size, I don't know. Because of its velocity, it now appears that Earth is directly in its elliptical path. Our best calculation, if the speed remains consistent, is that impact could come in two weeks." Several murmurs were heard throughout the room.

Dr. Patrick returned to the microphone. "Ladies and gentlemen, we need to alter this comet's path. The floor is open to any of your questions and suggestions."

A scientist from Lawrence Livermore Laboratory spoke first. "Obviously, we have a time factor here and the use of mirrors to reduce the size of this comet is a moot point. If we set up a kinetic impact, whatever we throw in the comet's path will have to be at least five thousand times its mass to have any effect. Anything less will be like a bug on a windshield. There is the possibility, though, of doing an internal detonation."

Mark Durham from the Space Science Institute interjected, "Internal detonation could cause fragmentation and thereby creating the same situation as the Shoemaker-Levy 9 Comet on Jupiter. The cure could be worse than the disease."

General Richards spoke next. "I suppose it comes from training, but when I see the enemy coming at me, my first response is to hit. Not being a scientist, I'm at a disadvantage, but if this comet could be hit by several nuclear bombs, wouldn't the remaining fragments be so small that they would simply burn up in the atmosphere before they did any damage to the earth?"

President Hewell asked, "What would be the wave-effect back to Earth from several nuclear bombs going off at once?"

Dr. Ellison Wong from MIT answered, "It depends on how far out we can hit it. When a nuclear bomb blasts through matter, the energy causes damage, but when it passes through air, it begins to dissipate. The further away from Earth it is, the more the blast effect becomes nil. We should, however, still be concerned with the electromagnetic pulse."

"Before we get involved with nuclear bombs, what about the push effect?" Dr. Kim Ming from UCLA asked.

Dr. Wong answered, "The payload and rocket would have to be huge for this size of comet. Unfortunately, we have nothing that I know of that would begin to stand up to this mass. It would be like trying to stop a Mack truck with a tricycle."

"It might be possible to create an artificial debris cloud to deflect its path," Dr. Cinzski from the Polish Space Office suggested. "But the concern is the size of this comet and experimentations to determine how large a cloud to create would be foolish and wasteful at this point."

"I have to agree with Dr. Cinzski," President Hewell said. "We must go with our best knowledge and not rely on experiments. We don't have the time. I feel that we have no choice but to go with nuclear warheads or ICBMs and be ready to go as soon as the comet is in range."

"And if the missiles miss the comet?" Dr. Ming asked.

"Then our only hope is prayer," the president answered quietly.

CHAPTER FORTY

D espite their attempts to keep the press away from the meeting at the Aerospace Corporation, Reuters managed to partially uncover the story. By Wednesday morning they had distributed the news to every major outlet in the world. The official report said, 'Comet Wilson coming perilously close to Earth. Visible only through a telescope now—should be visible in the night sky within a week when it's estimated to be approximately three hundred thousand miles out. Scientists are gearing up for big event.'

Amanda had just finished blow-drying her hair when she heard the WNN News Alert. She went to her bedroom television and turned up the volume."...Comet Wilson, the largest ever recorded." Dave Markham said. "For more on this story, we are joined by Dr. Isaac Beneke from the Mount Wilson Observatory in California. Dr. Beneke, what can you tell us about this comet? Is this a cause for alarm?"

"Not a cause for alarm, but a cause for concern. A comet the size of Comet Wilson, were it to hit Earth, would do immeasurable damage. However, comets, due to their elliptical paths, historically come near Earth, but not to Earth. Asteroids are the greater danger. The odds of an asteroid hitting Earth are once every five hundred thousand years, whereas the odds of a comet hitting Earth are once every thirty-two million years."

"How close do you estimate Comet Wilson will come to Earth?"

"A great deal depends on the speed of this comet. Presently, I would say it will not come closer than three hundred thousand miles. If, however, Comet Wilson increases its velocity there is the possibility that it could come as close as two hundred thousand miles, which would make this comet visible to the naked eye. The show would be spectacular."

Spectacular indeed, thought Amanda as she turned off the TV. Suddenly, a frightening thought crossed her mind. Could the angel sightings and this comet be somehow tied together?

CHAPTER FORTY-ONE

The cool morning fog clung to the Santa Inez Mountains as preparations were made for the missile launch at Vandenberg Air Force Base in California. Six Atlas missiles, loaded with nuclear warheads, were in position as scientists mathematically calculated the speed, distance, and impact time with the comet.

"General Richards," Dr. Patrick said as he closed his cell phone. "I've just spoken with Dr. Hoshiwara in El Segundo. We're going to have to launch much sooner than we planned. The comet has now increased speed to ninety-six kilometers per second."

"How much sooner?"

"At this rate, impact is expected on Tuesday. Our only window is Friday."

"That only gives us two days. Can we reprogram everything by then?"

"We have to," Dr. Patrick answered with urgency.

"All right then. I'll call the president."

CHAPTER FORTY-TWO

There was stillness in the air as dark clouds gathered over the Ngong Hills. Matu, clad in the traditional red toga of the Maasai, sniffed the air. It didn't smell like rain, and yet something was not right. He had an overwhelming feeling of danger, not unlike the time a pride of lions encircled the herd, and he and his brother had to fight them off with spears.

Sadly, that day, the lions claimed three of their precious cows and the tribe suffered for their loss. Matu blamed himself for not being more vigilant, and he swore to his father that it would never happen again. He scanned the savannah, carefully looking for any sign of movement, yet all was calm. Still, the ominous feeling would not leave him.

"Tumaini," he called to his younger brother. "Gather the cattle. We need to get them back to the pen."

Tumaini grabbed his spear and immediately began to herd the cattle back toward the enkang, the thorny enclosure that surrounded their village. He had learned long ago to trust his brother without question. His survival in the bush depended on it. The sky darkened as they finally secured the last of the cattle.

"Matu, why are you here so early?" his eight-year-old brother, Kanoro, asked. "Were there lions?"

"No," Matu replied as he latched the gate. He quickly glanced up at the sky and turned to go into the hut. He stopped, though, when he heard thunder.

Kanoro's eyes grew big. "Matu, what is that?" The sound grew louder, and the rumble was felt in the earth.

Jabet ran from the hut holding one-year-old Nanau. "What was that noise?"

Trying to discern what it was, Matu said nothing.

The vibrations and rumblings grew louder yet, and the earth shook. Then a quiet came over the land. Out of the stillness, a voice boomed from the heavens:

"Be Still…and know that I am God.
The God of Jesus,
The God of Abraham,
The God of Jacob,
The One God—The Only God.
Your hatred, Your disobedience,
And your greed are destroying you.
Prepare,
There is little time left."

The Maasai fell to their knees in fear.

Amanda was in the elevator when the lights finally flickered back on and it once again began its ascent. "Did you hear that?" Amanda asked as she looked at the others.

"What is this, some kind of a joke?" a young man asked from the back of the elevator.

"Pretty elaborate joke," another said.

The door opened on the sixteenth floor and Amanda walked into chaos at WNN.

.   .   .

The rocket guidance computers at Vandenberg Air Force Base rebooted again as the shaken operators tried to understand what they'd just heard.

"My God," said one technician. "What was that?"

"The data's gone," another said, racing into the control room. "It's all gone."

"But the launch…the comet…"

"It's too late. There's nothing we can do now."

CHAPTER FORTY-THREE

Comet Wilson, hovering ominously, was now clearly visible in the daytime. At night it was as bright as the full moon. It had been ten days since God had spoken. The world watched and waited. An eerie calm settled over old conflicts as people made peace with themselves and with God. President Hewell, and other heads of state, ordered all troops home. There was even peace, at last, in the Middle East. Churches, and synagogues were filled to capacity, and prayers could be heard throughout the world.

WNN was down to a skeleton crew, since many at the network decided to stay home with their families. Pete had returned to Mexico and April was at home with her mother. Even Martin Scolesco made amends with his estranged daughter and finally met his three grand-daughters.

Mark came into Amanda's office holding two cups of cappuccino piled high with whipped cream. "I figure we might as well enjoy ourselves."

Amanda smiled softly as she took a sip and cradled the warm cup in her hands. She looked up at him. "Mark, I've got to go home. Dad needs me. David and I are all he has."

His eyes were filled with sadness. "I know." He went over to her desk, gently pulled her up and enclosed her in his arms. He hugged her tightly, knowing this may be the last time he would hold her. He had to let her know how much she meant to him. "Amanda," he whispered in her ear, "I love you. I have since the first moment I met you."

She pulled back and looked into his eyes. "Mark, I love you, too, and I don't want to leave you. Please, come with me. If this world is going to end, let's be together."

"You're right, there's nowhere else I'd rather be than with you. I'll arrange the flights. Go home and pack what's important. I'll meet you back at your apartment."

Within the hour, Amanda was packed and ready to go. The thought of finally going home both excited and concerned her. There were many things she needed to resolve with her father, but now she was ready. Why had it taken her so long? Stubbornness, maybe. Pride, absolutely. Her father was a good man, and she was so happy he was going to meet Mark. She knew her father would love him as much as she did. For the first time in her life, she found someone who truly completed her. Even if they only had moments left on this earth, she wanted to be with him.

A knock on the door interrupted her thoughts. When she opened it, she immediately hugged Mark and then pulled back, feeling something was wrong. "What's the matter?"

"Flights are full, Amanda. Some of the airlines have even shut down since there's no one to man them."

"So we're not going?"

"No, you're going. There's one seat left on a flight leaving in two hours."

"No," she said loudly. "I'm not going without you."

"Yes, you are. You said it yourself. Your father needs you. I'm coming as soon as I can get there. There's a possibility of a seat on Friday. But you need to go now. This may be your only opportunity."

Amanda knew he was right, but the thought of leaving without Mark was more than she could bear. Tears began to fall as she hugged him. "Call me. If you can't reach me, I'll give you my dad's number and David's number at St. Teresa's." She pulled back and looked at Mark. His eyes were also welling with tears. "Friday then?" she asked. "You're coming on Friday?"

"I'll be there, Amanda. I promise," he whispered.

CHAPTER FORTY-FOUR

At Bethany Baptist Church, Mary Beth Hodges sat in the front pew next to Ellie LeBeaux as they quietly waited for Pastor Thomas to finish his silent prayer. At last, he raised his head and slowly walked to the pulpit.

"Brothers and sisters," he said with a smile as he raised his arms. "Today is a joyous day. We gather together in the love of God. We have heard His mighty voice and we know that He loves us. He loves us so much that He has given us a great gift, and that is the gift of salvation. All He has asked in return is that we love Him, that we keep His commandments, and that we love each other."

He leaned forward on the pulpit and clasped his hands. "We are all very aware of the fact that over the past several years, our world has become very secularized. Many people have chosen to ignore God and to live by their own rules. They have chosen hate over love. They have chosen to eliminate God wherever they can—in our schools, in our organizations, in our cities, and in our states. They say it is their rights they are trying to protect, when in reality it is simply that God's rules interfere with their own desires.

"Many of the people leading this fight choose not to believe in God at all. They claim He is a myth and that teaching the Bible is old-fashioned. People now know that God is not only real, but that He has not been happy with the way people have behaved. I said in the beginning that this is a joyous day—and it is! How can I say this when the world is so frightened? Because I believe that God is giving the entire world a second chance at salvation. He loves us so much that He wants us to be with Him, yes, even the enemy, if they give up their own self-love and turn to Him. God did not promise us eternal life on Earth, but He did promise us eternal life in heaven, if we believe. Brothers and sisters, have faith that God loves you."

CHAPTER FORTY-FIVE

Flight 235 to Portland was filled to capacity, so Amanda sat between two men in the back of the plane. It was eerily quiet as people read, slept, or just stared out the window at Comet Wilson, still hovering ominously. The plane touched down at twelve thirty. Outside security, Amanda saw her father waiting for her. Although still handsome, she immediately noticed that the years and the tiredness were beginning to show on his face. When at last he spotted her, his whole demeanor changed, and his face lit up in a smile. He put his arms out as Amanda approached him.

"Welcome home, Amanda," he said as he gave her a bear hug. "I've really missed you."

"Me too, Dad," she said, hugging him back, and this time she truly meant it.

"Have you had lunch?"

Amanda shook her head.

"Great," he said, "then I have a surprise for you. Do you feel like going on a picnic?"

Amanda brightened. "A picnic? What a great idea."

"And where's your favorite place?"

Amanda thought for a moment. "Rex Hill?"

"Exactly," he said. "I have everything in the car waiting. Fried chicken, corn on the cob—all your favorites."

She smiled, "Sounds wonderful."

"David's going to join us around three o'clock, but I thought we'd go right away. It will give us a chance to talk first."

They drove west on Highway 99 toward the wine country and turned right into the long, curving, flower-lined driveway. At last, they saw their destination. Off to the right was the imposing tile-roofed winery. The patios were laden with flowers—some in hanging baskets and others in pots. Straight ahead was the vineyard, where row after row of chardonnay and pinot vines were being carefully tended by the workers. Finally, off to the left, was the picnic area. The grass-covered terraces held tables and trellises covered with flowers.

"It's so beautiful," Amanda said. "I'd love to bring Mark here."

"Mark? Well, Amanda, we do have a lot of catching up to do."

After purchasing a bottle from the tasting room, they set up their picnic.

"It's been a long time, hasn't it?" he asked as he opened the wine and poured each of them a glass. "I've missed you so much."

"I've missed you too," Amanda said quietly. She looked down at her wine and ran her fingers around the glass. She then looked up into his eyes. "It's been my fault, Dad—this distance that's been between us. I don't know why. I guess as a kid I was just a natural rebel." Amanda noticed her father's smile, and she laughed softly. "Yeah, I know, but that was just part of who I was. It drove me crazy having anyone tell me what to do—especially if I thought they were trying to cram something down my throat that I didn't believe."

"Maybe I was a little hard on you…"

Amanda cut him off. "No, you weren't. You're a loving father who tried his best to raise his children to be good people and to love God. No, it was me. I was angry at God, I guess, for taking Mom away. I couldn't believe that a loving God would take a mother from her children, and at the same time, let so many bad things happen in the world. Then, I decided somewhere along the way that if this was the kind of God he was, I just didn't want any part of him."

Amanda's father gave her a look of understanding but kept silent as she continued, "Going to church was miserable for me. I watched you and David as you went forward to communion and I thought, how can you do this? How can you forgive a God who has hurt us so much and who obviously doesn't care about us? And yet, it amazed me that you and David were both so unwavering in your faith. I knew it was unfair of me, but I was so frustrated with you, and even more frustrated with David, who wanted to give his life to God. I just couldn't understand it. I needed to find out some answers for myself. That's why I was so anxious to leave home."

"So, have you come up with any answers?" her father asked.

"I think so," she answered. "No, that's not true. I know I have. You're right though, I've always been a skeptic. I have to see something to truly believe it. There are those who can believe without seeing, but I'm not one of them. Maybe that's why I fit in so well with the journalistic world. We always need facts to substantiate a story. I needed to see proof of God and I never did and so it was difficult for me to believe, until recently. It's strange how life works out, isn't it? As a journalist, my secular reporting of all the evils in the world has brought me full circle, to God," she continued, half surprised with the realization. She paused a moment to take a sip of wine, surprised that she was revealing more of herself than she ever intended.

"I know that your mother's death was hard on you," her father said after a moment. "It was hard on us all, but especially hard on you. She loved you so much. I suppose there's a special bond between mothers and daughters. I just wanted to help you so much, but I didn't know how to reach you. The only thing that got me through that difficult time was my faith. I thought that was what you needed, too. I suppose I was pretty rigid about everything, and I'm sorry about that."

"No, Dad, you were right. I told you that on the phone. The Ten Commandments are commandments, not suggestions, as you said. If everyone would just follow them, the world wouldn't be in this state today." She looked up at the comet, then back to her father, and reached out and touched his hand. "You are such a good person. I know God has to love you, and I do too, Dad."

Her father wiped a tear from his eye, looked off toward the vineyard for a moment, then turned back toward Amanda. "Do you know how proud I am of you?" he said. Amanda looked up at him and smiled. "And your mother would be, too," he continued. "As sad as the world is today, I'm happily looking forward to seeing your mother again. We had a wonderful marriage, Amanda, with you two beautiful children." He smiled at her and then became more serious. "I wanted the same thing for you, love and marriage and children." Amanda's sadness was apparent as she looked away, watching the breeze blow through the tops of the fir trees that lined the vineyard.

He reached over and held her hand, "Tell me about Mark. He has to be an exceptional man if you're interested in him."

Amanda told him everything about Mark, from his losing his family in the car accident to their relationship at work. She told him about what a wonderful journalist he was and how much they had in common. Finally, she told him about their realization that they were more than just friends and that everything felt so right.

"That's how your mom and I started out, you know. We were friends first, best friends, in fact. We always knew that we'd stay together forever because, if we lost each other, we would also lose our best friend. It sounds like that's what you have with Mark."

"I do," she whispered. "He's coming Friday and I can't wait to have you meet him. You'll love him, Dad. He reminds me of you." They turned as they heard a car drive up. It was David. Amanda checked her watch. It was already three o'clock. Time had passed so quickly. Both Amanda and her father went over to greet him and help him with all the food he had brought.

Friday morning, Amanda was so excited. Seeing Mark was all she could think about. She hadn't heard from him since the night she arrived in Portland. He had called to make sure she was safe and to say that he loved her and couldn't wait to see her on Friday. Wondering what time he would arrive, she called his cell phone, but there was no answer. Perhaps he was already in the air, she thought. The day was agonizingly long and by four o'clock she still hadn't heard from him. She again called his cell phone, then the studio. There was no answer at either number. Where is he? She closed her cell phone and tossed it on the sofa.

Her father came in and saw her frustration. "No word yet?"

"I can't get an answer anywhere."

"He'll be here, Amanda," her father said patiently.

"How do you know? What if something happened to him?"

"You just have to have faith."

There was no word from Mark on Friday, and by Saturday Amanda was getting worried. By Saturday night, she was beginning to fear that he wasn't coming. Her father came into her bedroom as she sobbed into her pillow. He rubbed her back and sat with her for a moment, not saying anything. She sat up and looked at him with tears still rolling down her cheeks.

"Something's happened. He's not coming. Oh Dad, we've wasted so much time, and now it's too late," she said as fell into his arms.

"Things aren't always what they seem, Amanda."

"Do you think he just changed his mind?"

"I don't know," her father said softly. "But until you hear bad news, don't borrow trouble. I know it's not easy, but this is the time you really need to have faith."

Amanda sat up and wiped her eyes. She took a deep breath. "You're right. I know you're right."

"Okay," he said as he stood. "Why don't you try to get some sleep? When he calls, I promise I'll come get you. But you need to get some rest. You haven't slept in two days."

He started to leave, and then turned back to Amanda. "Would you like to go to church with me tomorrow?"

She gave a slight smile. "Yes," she said softly.

He returned her smile. "Good. We'll leave about eight. Try to get some sleep."

CHAPTER FORTY-SIX

The glow of the ever-present comet filtered through the dark clouds as they drove to St. Theresa Catholic Church the following morning. Being there was strange for Amanda. Although she had not been in a church in years, she felt a comfortable familiarity, like she was coming home. As they entered the narthex, Amanda's father touched the holy water and crossed himself. At an empty pew, they knelt before the cross, moved toward the middle, then joined the congregation kneeling in silent prayer.

The mighty pipe organ began the processional hymn. The congregation watched as the censer-bearer with burning incense led the acolytes with the cross and candles, a deacon carrying the book of Gospels, and finally, Father David, slowly to the altar. There, he reverently bowed, kissing the altar cloth. He waited for the hymn to finish and then turned to the congregation.

"Let us pray. Our Heavenly Father, we humble ourselves before You today and ask for Your mercy." David paused a moment before he continued. "We know we have sinned against You and sinned against our brothers and sisters. We know this was not Your divine plan for us. You have loved us dearly and have given us so much, and rather than accepting these as wonderful gifts from You, our egos made us believe that we were the ones responsible for creating our fortunes, and even further, that it was our right to have so much. Along the way, many laid Your rules aside, because those rules interfered with their greed. Despite this, You have continued to love us all. The world has been so very wrong and we deeply apologize. Please, dear Lord, forgive us for our selfishness and show us mercy and strength in the days ahead. Amen."

The woman in front of Amanda dabbed her eyes with her handkerchief. Her husband reached for her, first lightly touching her hair, and then putting his arm around her to comfort her. Amanda knelt beside her father as David led the congregation in The Lord's Prayer.

"...Give us this day, our daily bread and forgive us our trespasses as we forgive those who trespass against us and lead us not into temptation, but deliver us from evil. Amen."

Amanda lifted her head with tears in her eyes as the Mass continued. She didn't want to die. There was so much more to do in life. She wanted children. She wanted Mark's children, and she loved him more than she ever thought possible, and now she feared it would never happen. She looked up as rain began pelting the stained glass windows.

"Peace of the Lord be with you," David said as he held up his arms.

"And also with you," the congregation responded.

She turned to her father and hugged him.

"Peace be with you, Amanda," he said softly.

"Peace, Dad," she whispered back.

Communion took longer than ever before, as each person knelt at the altar to receive the sacrament. Many stayed kneeling at the rail as they looked up at the cross and said silent prayers. Some parishioners looked up at David with tears in their eyes. David stopped to comfort them and prayed for their strength in the coming days.

The rain was coming down harder now. At the end of the Mass, David once again held up his arms and raised his voice to be heard over the din. "Let us pray. Lord, you are the source of eternal health for those who believe in you. May our brothers and sisters who are refreshed with food and drink from heaven safely reach your kingdom of light and life. We ask this through Christ our Lord." David raised his head and said to the congregation. "The Mass has ended. Go in peace to love and eternally serve the Lord."

The parishioners filed silently out of the church, with Amanda and her father at the end of the line. As Amanda approached David she gave him a hug. "I love you," she whispered.

"I love you, too, Amanda," he replied softly.

She watched David hug their father, then glanced at the parishioners wanting prayers forming a line in the narthex. "I'm needed here right now, but I'll be back to the house later," he said.

"Of course," he said. "We'll see you soon."

He turned to Amanda. "It's really raining out there. Let me bring the car around."

"No, I'm fine," Amanda said, as she took his arm and slowly walked out with him into the storm. Her tears mixed with the rain.

"You okay?" he asked once they were settled in the car.

Amanda wiped her eyes. "Are any of us okay? We're all going to die."

"God is good, Amanda. We don't have a vengeful God. He loves us. If He decides that this is our time to join him in heaven, then He has good plans for us. You just have to have faith."

"I've tried Dad. I just wanted to see Mark one last time. Is that too much to ask?" She sat there in silence for a few moments as rain continued to pound the windshield. "I'm sorry. I know I'm acting like a child."

"Apologies aren't necessary. I know how you feel. If I could have seen your mother just one more time..." His voice trailed off. "But now, I feel like God is answering my prayer. I know I'll see her, just as I know you'll see Mark. We aren't brought into this world to live forever, Amanda. Just as I'm delighted to have you and David with me right now, God wants us with Him as well."

Amanda was quiet as she thought about what he said. Will she see Mark again? Her immediate thought was yes. Was that thought a hope or was it the faith that her Dad was talking about? She asked her Dad, "How do you know it's really faith, rather than a hope?"

"That's the easy part," he said "Hope is a maybe, but faith is a definite yes in your mind," he said as he slowed to turn a corner. "You've been on a lot of assignments. Were you ever worried that some of them would put you in a bad position?"

"Not really. No"

"Why?"

Thinking back, Amanda finally said, "I guess it's because I thought things through first. I prepared, so hopefully very few things could go wrong."

"Then putting your mind in the right place gave you a strong advantage over just a hope and therefore your mind was in a position of having faith in your decision."

"I guess you could say that. But what about things you can't control? Where does faith enter into it?"

"It's the same," he said. You do everything you can. You make plans. Your mind is right. It's no longer just a hope, it's a plan and that's where faith comes in. Now you're waiting for the final resolution with faith. It goes beyond hope and that's where God comes in. God loves faith, and quite often helps out in the final resolutions."

"It always comes back to God," Amanda mused.

"It always does," he agreed. "He's the Father who wants to help His child."

Amanda gave her Dad a smile. "Thanks for helping me."

"Any time," he responded, as he turned down his street. The rain continued to pour, obscuring the trees and houses. As he drove closer to the house, there was a figure on the porch. He pulled into the driveway and, without saying a word, Amanda quickly let herself out of the car. "Mark," she yelled and raced to his open arms.

He was cold, wet, unshaven, and his clothes were wrinkled from days of travel, but he was there. She couldn't believe it. She hugged him tightly. "Where have you been? Are you okay?" she asked as she pulled back and touched his bristly face. "What happened?"

"It's a long story," he said, hugging her again. "But I'm here. I promised. We're together. That's the most important thing."

Amanda's father came up the steps. "You must be…"

"Mark! "Amanda almost shouted with joy.

"James Fox," he said, extending his hand.

Mark clasped his hand. "Sir, it's a pleasure to meet you."

"Come in out of the rain," James said. "How about a hot cup of coffee?"

"Perfect," Mark replied.

Amanda lit a fire while her dad was busy making coffee. Within minutes, she joined Mark on the sofa, and her father emerged with a tray filled with a pot, four cups and small plates, and another over-flowing with cookies.

"There we go," her father said, setting the tray down. Amanda poured coffee as James sat in his leather chair. "We've heard a lot about you, Mark," he said. We're so glad you made it."

"Yes," Amanda said. "What happened?"

"Well," Mark started. "As you know, flights were booked solid. Actually, over sold. I did score a seat on Friday, but I overheard a flight attendant telling a man, who was an employee of the airline and was traveling non rev, that he had to give up his seat. He was with his family and his wife was understandably upset, so I gave him my tick-et." Amanda glanced at her father and saw a small smile. "I figured I'd drive my car. Unfortunately, everyone else had the same idea. Traffic was close to a stand-still on the freeways. Plus, hotels were totally booked. So, I inched across the country and slept, as well as I could, in the car. Along the way, I met a couple who had car trouble and were anxious to get to Omaha where her family lived. They were nice and helped me with driving. They slept in the back and I slept in the front."

"Good grief," Amanda said. "I was so worried. Why didn't you call?"

"Couldn't. Even between the three of us, all the phones were dead. Did try the phone at their Omaha house, but their power had been down as well. I figured the best thing was to just keep going. Oh, I didn't mention that with so many people on the road, that gas stations put a limit of 10 gallons per vehicle. For those with electric vehicles, they were really out of luck because of the power outages along the way." He looked around the house. "Have you had problems with losing power?"

"No," James said. "I don't know why, but we've been fortunate."

"Anyway, you made it. Thank you, God, " Amanda said.

They all looked up as David came through the door. Amanda jumped up and gave her brother a hug. "Mark, this is my brother David."

Mark stood and extended his hand. "Father, so nice to meet you."

"And we're delighted to finally meet you," David said, clasping Mark's hand.

"Listen," David said as he ran toward the window and saw that the rain was beginning to ease. A strange quiet filled the skies. James opened the front door and stood on the porch as the others joined him. Other neighbors began to venture outside as all watched the sky and waited.

Then, they all heard something off in the distance. It was the same low rumbling the world had heard before—a distant rumbling that came closer and grew louder by the moment. The vibrations from the earth sent many to their knees. David and his father came closer to Amanda and Mark as they all looked up.

People everywhere were tearfully praying and holding one another, knowing that their time had finally come. Agonizing moments passed as they awaited their fate.

Then thunder boomed through the heavens. The earth rumbled loudly, then a deafening silence fell upon them. The seconds seemed like hours as they waited.

Finally, the voice of God filled the heavens:

"My children, I have heard your prayers.
I have watched you turn your hatred into Love;
Your greed into Charity;
Your evil ways into Good.
I have witnessed your Faith

And I am Pleased."

Another thunderous boom echoed through the sky and the storm clouds slowly parted, revealing a brilliantly blue sky. Miraculously, Comet Wilson was no longer there.

"I love you and will be with you always."

The End

"The nations raged, the kingdoms moved,
But when His voice was heard,
The troubled earth was stilled to peace
Before His mighty Word.
The Lord of Hosts is on our side,
Our safety is secure,
The God of Jacob is for us
A refuge strong and sure"

— *ORIGINAL TRINITY HYMNAL NO. 37, PSALM 46*

NOTE FROM THE AUTHOR

I hope you enjoyed *Be Still—And Know That I Am God.*

Like to share this message with other readers?

I would sincerely appreciate your scanning the QR code below and leaving a review:

Thank You!

OTHER WORKS BY PAMELA YOUNG

Jericho's Wall

The Healing

Natural Healing Foods

Available on Amazon Kindle

and at:

PamelaYoungBooks.com

Group and bulk quantities available

www.ingramcontent.com/pod-product-compliance
Lightning Source LLC
Chambersburg PA
CBHW020631180626
46816CB00003B/911